About the Author

Paul Devito was raised in Italy until the age of nine and then in upstate New York. He studied and taught at a college in Syracuse and then learned how to paint. He has written several novels.

The Statue at Dawn

Paul Devito

The Statue at Dawn

Olympia Publishers
London

www.olympiapublishers.com
OLYMPIA PAPERBACK EDITION

Copyright © Paul Devito 2024

The right of Paul Devito to be identified as author of
this work has been asserted in accordance with sections 77 and 78 of
the Copyright, Designs and Patents Act 1988.

All Rights Reserved

No reproduction, copy or transmission of this publication
may be made without written permission.
No paragraph of this publication may be reproduced,
copied or transmitted save with the written permission of the publisher,
or in accordance with the provisions
of the Copyright Act 1956 (as amended).

Any person who commits any unauthorised act in relation to
this publication may be liable to criminal
prosecution and civil claims for damage.

A CIP catalogue record for this title is
available from the British Library.

ISBN: 978-1-80439-431-1

This is a work of fiction.
Names, characters, places and incidents originate from the writer's
imagination. Any resemblance to actual persons, living or dead, is
purely coincidental.

First Published in 2024

Olympia Publishers
Tallis House
2 Tallis Street
London
EC4Y 0AB

Printed in Great Britain

Dedication

I dedicate this book to my mother.

Chapter One

The hills surrounding Florence were bathed in sunlight. We had been traveling from a small town two hours south of the city. Sixty-five of us were spending our final year of college in Italy to study the Renaissance and learn about Italian culture. The two buses barely fit in the narrow streets of Florence, and our eyes were darting in every direction, soaking up the sights. The tan and orange buildings were bright in the afternoon light, and the pedestrians were hurrying home from work.

I was sitting next to a young woman named Monica, whom I had met on the plane from New York. She had long blonde hair, braided in a tail, big blue eyes, and a coy smile. She was slender and spoke vivaciously. Monica and I had both spent a few years of our childhood living in Italy, because our fathers were Italian. She was an artist, very confident and talented, as I would find out later. She had the window seat on the bus, so I had an excuse to stare at her as I looked out the window. We shared stories of our childhood and the culture shock we experienced every time we traveled to Europe.

"Do you have a boyfriend in the States?" I asked.

"Sort of, but we're just friends now; I didn't want to get too serious," she said.

"Do you want to get married and have children some day?" I said.

"Someday, perhaps, but there's so much I want to do before I settle down," she said.

I was glad to hear that. Nothing bothered me more than a

talented person who just wanted to get married at an early age. Monica was a challenge, so I didn't want her to think that I was interested in her; the game had begun, and I was already infatuated.

"What are your paintings like?" I asked.

"Impressionistic, I guess, but different. I don't really know how to describe them."

"I wish I could paint," I said.

"You can if you want to. It just takes some work. I'm sure you have enough talent."

"How do you know I have talent?" I asked her.

"You're Italian!" she laughed.

I loved to hear her laugh. It sounded so natural and so innocent. The buses pulled up to the hotel where we were all staying for three days of orientation. Everybody was very tired and relieved to have arrived. As we got off, I smelled the air and felt my childhood rushing back to me. I remembered running through the streets of Rome at the age of eight, fearless and untroubled. Tears filled my eyes as the memories flooded over me.

"It's great to be back, isn't it, Monica?" I said.

"Yeah, this is great," she said.

"After you unpack and everything, do you want to go out for a cappuccino?" I said.

"Sure, give me about an hour."

I went to my room, but decided not to unpack right away. Instead, I lay down on the bed and closed my eyes. I imagined kissing Monica on the Ponte Vecchio, as the moon hung over the river Arno. A few minutes later, the door opened and a guy named John walked in. I had seen him with our group, but I hadn't talked to him yet.

"Hi, I guess we're roommates for a couple of days," I said. "I'm Paul."

"I'm John. Nice to meet you."

John was about five feet ten and very well built. He looked like a football player. By comparison, I was delicately built. I had played tennis and basketball. John had a mustache and a quick smile. He was very friendly, and we got along well. John began unpacking right away, and even though I was very tired, I was too excited to sleep. He and I talked about New York City, where he lived, and about our childhood, among other things.

Our room was small, with twin beds separated by an antique table. The furnishings were sparse but elegant, and they were quite comfortable. A reproduction of DaVinci's Annunciation hung directly across from my bed; it made me think of my early years in Italian school, when DaVinci was one of my heroes.

In some ways, John was a typical New Yorker, tough, and quick witted. He had seen it all, and was much more mature than I in certain areas. Having grown up in Brooklyn, he had learned to survive by his wits. How he had managed to pay for his year in Italy I never found out, but I discovered he was extremely resourceful. John was street smart, whereas, I had not been exposed to the streets and had retained a good deal of my innocence.

After a long conversation with John, I went looking for Monica. I found her sleeping on her bed, her bags still packed. I woke her up, and although she was very tired, I talked her into going out for a coffee.

The downtown streets of Florence are always busy, and it was exciting just to walk along the narrow sidewalks. A café with tables outside was only a block away, and we were fortunate to find some seats.

"I can't get over the feelings I'm having just being here," I said.

"I know what you mean. It feels like I'm a child again," she said.

"You will be very inspired to paint while you're here," I said.

"You should do something artistic too. Have you thought about it?" she said.

"I don't talk about it much, but I'd like to become a writer," I said.

"What a perfect place to start," she said.

"I don't know where to start, really; I have some ideas, but as yet, I haven't put anything on paper," I said.

"Keep thinking about it; eventually something will come out," she said.

"Have you written anything?" I said.

"I wrote some poetry when I was in high school, you know? Junky love poems that didn't amount to much," she said, "but then I got into painting, and I haven't written anything since."

"I really don't think that I could paint, but I do think I could write," I said.

We sipped our coffee and chatted some more. Her eyes were lively with excitement, and I could feel myself falling for her. I played it cool, careful to mask my interest, but I was definitely infatuated. We walked back to the hotel and went to our own rooms. I was so tired; I got into bed right away.

Chapter Two

I didn't sleep well that night; I was so excited to be in Italy. At six o'clock in the morning, I woke up realizing that I wasn't going to get any more sleep. Then I decided to look for a café that was open. The one on the corner was closed, but a block down the street, a café was just opening up. My Italian was rusty, but I didn't have any trouble understanding the conversation around me. Italians have a particular sense of humor that usually includes a note of sarcasm. It seems built right into the language almost, so that everything has a tinge of humor, no matter how negative it might be. The proprietor was complaining about a late shipment of coffee, and he was making fun of the deliveryman at the same time. I could remember my father saying similar things, and I laughed to myself that nothing had changed.

I sat outside. The sun was just beginning to rise, and the smell and taste of the coffee carried an intense rush of memories. A few minutes later, John showed up. We sat together and talked about our pasts some more. Our stories were so different, but here we were in the same place, trying to learn about the Renaissance.

"Have you met Monica yet, John?"

"No, but I saw you talking to her. Are you in love?"

"I could be, I think; she's got a lot of interesting and beautiful qualities, but I don't think she's interested in me."

"Take your time; she might be interested in you but may

not be showing it," he said.

The hustle and bustle of the city was just beginning. It was exciting to watch the city wake up and come to life. We were sitting by the river, and I watched it change colors as the sun rose higher in the sky. I had two cappuccinos, which made me feel even more excited than I already was. After our coffees, we walked back to the hotel to find the others getting up slowly.

We didn't have to do much for orientation. They just wanted to keep us together for three days before they introduced us to our host families. I wanted to hang out with Monica the whole day, but I decided to cool it and get to know some of the others. About fifty women were in the program, versus ten guys: odds that I liked immensely.

John and I decided to go for a long walk through the city to explore our new home. I was overwhelmed with the beauty of the city. We headed for downtown; I wanted for see the Duomo, which is the largest church, right in the center of the city. The dome of the cathedral, built by Brummeleschi, is one of the great architectural achievements of all time. John and I talked a great deal, and began to establish a friendship that would grow closer as the year progressed. At lunchtime, we got a slice of pizza and sat outside one of the cafés.

"You must have your eye on one of the women," I said.

"I'm playing it cool for a while; I'm not choosing anybody until I get to know them a little better. There are quite a few beautiful ones though. Aren't there?" he said.

I thought his strategy sounded good, so I decided I would also try to play it cool for a while. My decision wasn't very steadfast as it turned out, because I began making moves toward Monica the very next day. John and I were exhausted by the time we got back to the hotel. We had a great dinner and I went to bed very early. I slept better that second night and felt very energetic the next morning.

On that second day, we were scheduled to meet our host families. I was hoping my family had a pretty daughter, but as it happened, they had two sons around my age. The sons came alone to the hotel to meet me, and I felt very fortunate that they were nice guys. The older one, Sergio, already had a receding hairline. He was short and thin with a handsome face. The younger brother, my exact age, was very handsome, a little taller than Sergio, and was named Riccardo.

Instantly, we became friends, and went to a café to get better acquainted. They were students as well, but were facing conscription into the army within the next couple of years. The two of them were so glad I spoke Italian, since they had sponsored students before that they couldn't communicate with. After chatting for a couple of hours, I went back to the hotel to look for Monica. She wasn't anywhere to be found, so I talked to a guy named Jesse, who would later become one of my close friends.

"What are you studying here?" I asked.

"Mostly the language and history," he said. "I'm going to law school."

"I'm thinking of going to law school too," I said, "but I haven't completely made up my mind. I might study English instead, and go into teaching."

"You speak Italian fluently, don't you?" he said.

"Yes, I spent five years of my childhood living in Rome and going to an Italian school. I'm interested in Renaissance literature and art," I said.

"I'm mostly interested in Italian women," he said. "I'll

study when I have to, but I want to immerse myself in the culture." He laughed.

"I know what you mean; they all wear those short skirts. My neck is getting sore from turning my head all the time," I said.

I felt sleepy again, not having caught up completely from the previous two nights, and I decided to take a nap. I only wanted to sleep for half an hour, but woke up two hours later, not knowing where I was. As I looked around the room at the antique furniture, I felt I was in my room at the age of eight. I got dressed and walked downstairs to socialize. Monica was talking to another woman. I didn't go over to her right away, but was planning to talk to her as soon as she was free. Many of the students had left the hotel to go sightseeing; only a few of us were around. A few minutes later, I spotted Monica going up to her room.

I wanted to follow her up there, but I decided I wouldn't, because I didn't want to make a nuisance of myself. It was about five in the evening. The sun was still hanging high in the sky when I walked out into the fresh air. My mood was elevated immediately as I strolled along the interesting shops. I walked to one of the bridges and just sat, watching a few fishermen try their luck. The water was muddy and reflected the buildings on the other side. I thought about Monica, then remembered what John had said about taking one's time. Then I walked to another coffee shop and listened to the conversations around me. The light reflecting off the street and houses made me think of some paintings I had seen. I thought about my childhood in Rome, the long afternoons playing soccer in the park, the days spent in Catholic school.

I realized I was truly a product of two cultures. Like the

Italians, I laughed and created laughter, never taking life too seriously. However, I was not hotheaded like my father, but rather calm and collected like my American mother. I wondered how much of my personality was genetic, and how much environmental, but this question couldn't be answered. It seemed I was an interesting combination of various qualities and experiences from several different towns and provinces. I felt comfortable enough being in Italy, but it didn't feel like home.

A woman from our program named Ellen walked by me, and I flagged her down. I had briefly spoken to her at the airport in New York and was attracted to her warm personality.

"Hey, Paul, what are you up to?" she said.

"Just daydreaming. I love being here; I feel like a kid again," I said.

"You and Monica must have a lot to talk about," she said winking.

"Yeah, we get along pretty well," I said.

"Do you want to walk along the river?" she asked.

"Sure," I said.

I finished my coffee and walked with her on the cobblestone street along the Arno. The sun reflected off the water in dazzled spots, reminding me of Renoir's impressionistic depiction of rivers. Everything was art, the buildings, the sky, the water, even the people. Ellen was very attractive. She had long, slender legs and a great ass. Her hair was long and light brown. She had big, sexy, brown eyes that sparkled with wit, but her best feature was her quick smile, which was warm with sensuality.

"Did you meet your Italian family?" I asked.

"I'm not exactly with a whole family; I'm renting a large

room from an older woman. It has its own entrance and kitchen," she said.

"That sounds like a great situation," I said.

"Yes, I'm really happy about it. You'll have to come over for dinner sometime."

"Anytime!" I said.

We walked for half an hour, until we got back to the hotel. I went to my room and fantasized about sleeping with Ellen. She had completely taken my mind off Monica.

After sleeping for a couple of hours, I joined the other students for dinner. We had pasta and a portion of pork with beans. In the evening, Jesse, John, and I went out to a club for young artists and students in general. They served beer and coffee. The place was small. It was in the basement of a building near the river, and they were playing American music, which was typical of many Italian nightspots.

The three of us ordered beers and sat in a corner where we could observe the rest of the small room. Neither of them had been to Italy before. They felt like kids at an amusement park.

"Look at that one," Jesse said, nodding toward a stunning dark haired woman.

"They're everywhere," John said.

"Notice that none of the women here are overweight, and their skin is so flawless," I said.

Most of the seats were taken, but there were two available at our table, so two of the women asked if they could sit with us. We said sure, and they noticed right away that we were Americans, which fascinated them. John and Jesse had studied Italian in school and were able to understand everything, even though they had trouble speaking.

One woman was named Laura, and the other was named Gabriela. Laura had long, dark, curly hair, fine features, and large brown eyes. Gabriela had short, curly, blonde hair and was taller than Laura. They were not shy at all and engaged us in conversation right away. Both of them were very curious about the States, and wanted to hear about New York City in particular.

John lived in the city and tried as hard as he could to describe it. Jesse and I had been to New York many times, and we helped John tell the women about it. We thought maybe we could get their phone numbers at the end of the evening, but they said no, and only told us to come back to the club other nights. We talked about the women all the way back to the hotel and collapsed on our beds with smiles on our faces.

Chapter Three

The next day we moved into our new homes, and I spent several hours talking to Riccardo and Sergio, after I had made my bed. I was living only a few blocks from the school in a small room with a window overlooking a wide avenue. During the day, the city streets were pretty loud, but in the evening it was very quiet. After unpacking, I went outside and walked around the neighborhood, familiarizing myself with my new surroundings. Right outside my apartment was a café, and I went there immediately to get a cappuccino. I decided to walk to school, in order to find the quickest way there. My route included walking over a little bridge and several tiny streets that made the city so interesting.

When I got to school, I ran into Ellen who had basically done the same thing I had. She told me she was living only a couple of blocks away from me, which I thought was very convenient.

"How do you like your room?" I asked.

"I love it. I have a little garden right outside my glass doors, and my landlady is the sweetest person," she said.

"Do you know where Monica is living?" I said.

"She's in the other direction," she said, pointing downtown, "about five blocks."

Ellen and I walked toward our new places, taking our time and enjoying the sights. I noticed that she was asking me many personal questions, which felt like an intense form of flirting.

Somehow we got on the subject of sex, and I was somewhat surprised when she asked me what my favorite position was.

"I like every position," I said. "The more variety, the better," I added, as if I had plenty of experience.

"I like doggy style," she said. "I can't orgasm in the missionary position."

"I wonder why they call it the missionary position," I said.

"Because missionaries have no imagination," she retorted quickly.

"Let's go to my place," she said. "I'll make you some coffee or tea."

Ellen had a beautiful, large room with antique furniture, and French doors overlooking the garden. It was ideal. She had a big kitchen on one side of the room, just large enough for one person to cook. Prints of various Renaissance painters decorated the wall. I was instantly jealous, because I had been placed in a tiny room. Later, I would be grateful, because I had two "brothers" who would often keep me company.

We were coffeed out, so she made us tea. We sat in the garden amongst the trees and plants. Our conversation had not let up since we had met at school, and I was starting to think that maybe we would become lovers.

"Do you have a boyfriend in the States?" I asked.

"Sort of. I don't know. We kind of broke up just before I left. I had fantasies of going out with Italian men," she laughed.

"You and I seem to have a lot to talk about," I said.

"Conversation flows easily between us. You're well educated. I like that," she added.

Several birds were flying around the garden, and I found myself watching them intently, enjoying their song. One day, many years later, I would write a book of poetry about birds, but little did I know then that I was fascinated by them. Ellen was wearing shorts. I kept sneaking peeks at her long, sensuous legs and let my fantasies go wild. Every once in a while, Monica would pop into mind, and I kept comparing the two women. After an hour of chitchat, I decided not to overstay my welcome and go home to see if Riccardo or Sergio were there. I gave her a kiss on the cheek as I left, and told her I would see her in school the next day.

I went to bed early and woke up refreshed. It was our first day of school in Italy and, to be truthful, I wasn't interested in anything I might learn. All I wanted to do was meet more women. I tried to dress like an Italian, sporting gray wool slacks and a light sweater over a dress shirt. Also, I decided to grow a beard as so many Italian men did. The school was buzzing with people when I arrived. I went right to the little café in our building and sat down with a cappuccino. That's when I met Horace.

Horace was the most interesting character of the bunch. He wasn't in our program. His wife was, and he had come along for the ride. He was from a poor southern family and had been a cook for several years. Horace was about twenty-six years old, short, with long hair. He was a pistol, and he said the most outrageous things, always with a twist of irony and a wry sense of humor. When it was just the two of us, he would tell me stories about women that I could hardly believe. Melanie, his third wife already, was quiet and intellectual, the complete opposite of Horace, who was loud and liked to entertain everybody.

He reminded me of Henry Miller in many ways. He had lived his stories; he wasn't just telling tales. The minute I walked into the café, he introduced himself. Even though he was not from a middle class family, he was not intimidated by people from different social classes and was confident that he had the wits to match anybody.

"Hi, I'm Horace, and this is my wife, Melanie," he said with an expansive smile.

"I'm Paul, and I'm still looking for a wife, I think."

"Melanie's my third wife," he said, "but I'm still looking too." He laughed.

"Third wife," I thought. "This guy must be crazy."

"I just said that to keep her on her toes," Horace added.

Several women were in the café, coming in and out of class, and I noticed Horace checking them all out. Melanie didn't seem surprised by anything Horace said. I guess she was used to him. When Ellen came in, I motioned her to sit with us. She was wearing a very short skirt with a tee shirt, and she looked great.

"What's up, kiddo?" I said.

"I've got modern Italian literature in a few minutes," Ellen said.

"So do I," I said.

"You guys read Italian?" Horace asked.

"Yes," we both said.

"I'm impressed," he said.

A few minutes later, Monica walked in. She stood at the bar and ordered a cappuccino. Ellen and I greeted her, and she joined us at our table. When she sat down, I noticed for the first and only time that Horace didn't say a word.

Monica and Ellen developed a special bond very quickly and would end up spending a lot of time together during the rest of the year. Monica wore very little makeup and dressed more conservatively than Ellen. She was wearing jeans and a nice blouse. She was studying studio art only, and had formulated her own schedule. Monica spent long hours in the studio and would venture out every hour or so for a cup of coffee.

While Ellen was talkative and outgoing, Monica was more reserved and chose to speak only when she felt she had something interesting or important to say. I discovered I was more easily able to open up to Ellen, who was not judgmental and was always very supportive. Monica was more intense and critical.

"What are you doing today?" Ellen asked Monica.

"We're sketching a live model for a couple of hours. Then I'm going downtown to shop," Monica said.

"I'll go with you," Ellen said.

I wanted to go with them, but I didn't say anything. I was trying to control my impulses. A dark haired young woman was standing at the bar, and I asked Horace who she was. Her name was Kristen, he told me, and she looked very Italian. A few minutes later, our group dispersed to attend class, and I sat down next to Kristen in our literature seminar. She smiled at me, and I introduced myself. I had trouble paying attention to our professor, because I was obsessed with looking at the various women in our class.

After class was over, I talked to Kristen for a while. I discovered she was a poet, and we hit it off immediately. She was nineteen and as gorgeous as Monica, only with dark eyes and hair and tanned skin. My head was spinning from falling in love with all the attractive women at the same time.

Kristen seemed more mature than the others, very pensive, and she only laughed gleefully on rare occasions. She was sweet and considerate and chose her words carefully. We talked about various writers for a long time. She knew much more about literature than I did, and I enjoyed learning from her. I hesitated to tell her that I wanted to become a writer, but finally, I confided in her. She was excited about the idea and was very encouraging. I told her some of my ideas and she thought they were pretty good.

I'll never forget her saying, "Just sit down and do it; don't let anyone or anything stop you."

It turned out that we were in three of the same classes, being humanities majors, and I respected her a great deal for her insightful contributions to class.

Kristen lived in my neighborhood as well, so I walked home with her. I brought her up to my room, which she wasn't too impressed with, but she met my "brothers" and agreed they were a great asset. We were sitting on my bed when I was overcome with passion, and I tried to kiss her. She let me kiss her for a minute, then pushed me away.

"I really like you, Kristen," I said, trying to kiss her again.

"Slow down, Paul. You don't even know me... I'm not going to jump into bed with you, if that's what you think."

"I don't think that!" I said. "I just want to make out with you and get more intimate. How do you think I'm going to know you better if I don't break down the walls a little?" I said.

"We can just talk. I'll tell you anything you want to know," she said.

"I want to know if you like me," I said.

"So far I like you," she said.

I was too excited and a little irrational when I decided, on the spur of the moment, just to take my pants off. She was shocked and said:

"What are you doing? Put your pants back on!"

I realized immediately that I had done the wrong thing and quickly pulled my pants up.

"Now I like you less." She laughed.

I was glad she took it as well as she did; I was disappointed in myself, but knew that my impulsiveness was due to not having had sex in a long time.

"I'm sorry, Kristen. I don't know what came over me!"

"I'm just irresistible," she said, and added, "by the way you have a nice cock."

"Thanks." I laughed.

Our nervous laughter subsided, and we talked for a little while, until she decided to leave. She didn't seem upset, which surprised me, but I felt foolish. I thought that the way she handled the situation might mean she really liked me after all, or she would have left in a huff. I went to bed that night with fantasies of Kristen and woke up the next morning with a huge erection.

Chapter Four

The next few days were filled with exploring the city. My "brother" Riccardo and I became close friends over the first few days, and he showed me places in and out of Florence that only natives knew about. One Saturday, Kristen and I walked up to Foesole, a town up in the hills overlooking the city. She picked flowers along the way, and I kept trying to kiss her every fifteen minutes. The pine trees in Italy are different from ours, and I kept looking at them, reminded of my childhood. Kristen and I didn't talk much on the way up the hill. I followed behind her, staring at her ass.

When she reached the town, we were too tired to walk around, so we sat at a café and had some coffee. I felt like we were getting close and decided to confide in her things that I told very few people.

"Do you know anything about mental illness, Kristen?" I said.

"I've been depressed before, but not too seriously. Why?" she said.

"I had a nervous breakdown when I was nineteen; there had been no sign of illness until six months prior to the breakdown, when I got very depressed for about three months. Then my mind rebounded and I got very manic, or high. I was running about ten miles a day and taking ten courses at Georgetown, when my brain first fizzled, and I ended up in the hospital for a few months."

"That must have been awful," she said, "but you seem to have recovered nicely."

"I was fortunate. The medication they have today is miraculous, and I was brought right back to my senses. I had to wait a year to go back to school, but my mind was very focused when I returned."

She had a very empathetic look on her face, and I was glad I had confided in her.

"I have pretty violent mood swings myself," she said, "but so far I haven't gone off the deep end."

"I don't tell too many people about my breakdown," I said.

"I feel honored that you told me, and don't worry, I won't tell anyone else," she said.

We finished our coffee and walked around the town a little bit. She seemed happy, and I was feeling in love. At one point, while we were walking down a narrow street, I put my arm around her, and we walked that way for a few minutes. She seemed comfortable with me; we were both poets. Though I didn't know it at the time, we seemed to share a certain intense sensitivity. Language flowed freely between us, and we never had trouble understanding each other. I asked her about previous boyfriends; she told me she had really only had two who had been quite different from each other. Neither of them had worked out.

We descended the hill back to Florence and went our separate ways. I had never felt so much in love in my life; I imagined I was walking two feet above the ground. I returned to my apartment and told Riccardo and Sergio how I felt. They both wanted to meet women in our program, so we decided to go to school together the next day.

Horace was laughing and talking up a storm when I entered the café in the morning. I introduced him to my "brothers," but they couldn't communicate because of the language barrier. I let Sergio and Riccardo take care of themselves, and I sat down next to Horace. Melanie was in class, so Horace and I could talk man to man. He liked to shock me with his stories, and that morning he told me about a time when he had been young and reckless. His friends and he had been drinking heavily and were sitting in the middle of a country road in the depths of Georgia. Very rarely did a car go by, but that evening, a young woman was driving down that road and had to stop because they were in her way. They pulled her out of the car, dragged her into the woods, and raped her. He had no compunction telling me this story, and I had not doubt that it was true.

I looked around to make sure that nobody had heard him, but Horace wasn't the least bit concerned. Even though I wasn't too thrilled to hear that story, he told it in such a way that it just seemed almost normal. I laughed about it, and asked him to tell me another one. His stories so impressed me that I missed my first two classes. Kristen came into the café and reminded me that I was in school. I went to my political science class, but I kept thinking about Horace's stories.

Kristen and I went out for lunch to a little trattoria around the corner. The pasta was very inexpensive and was made fresh, so we quickly made it our place to go, and it wasn't long before the proprietor recognized us as regulars. We decided to skip our afternoon classes and go to a church not far away to see the stained glass windows and some fourteenth century frescoes.

Walking into the church felt like we were being transported into the past. Candles lighted the frescoes, but there were small spotlights as well. Kristen sat down in the first pew and took out her notebook. She wrote for a while, taking her time, looking at the walls, and glancing over at me from time to time. I asked her if I could read what she was writing, but she wouldn't let me. Gazing at the frescoes, all I could think of was how much art had changed, how secular it had become, and how many more varieties had been developed. After the church, we went to Kristen's house, where an elderly couple lived and Kristen had her own large room.

As soon as Kristen closed the door to her room, she took me in her arms and kissed me. We kissed and kissed and kissed, until my lips were about to fall off. She let me put my hand up her skirt and under her panties, but she wouldn't touch me.

"Not yet," she whispered.

I felt exhilarated being with her; her lips were so tender, and her eyes so beautiful. I wanted to make love to her, and I told her so, but she wanted me to be patient. We made out for a couple of hours, every so often coming up for a breath of air. At that age, I fell in love every month, and I was convinced I was in love with Kristen.

At one point, while taking a breather, I asked her if she loved me.

"Not yet, silly," she said, trying to kiss me again.

Even though she was several years younger than I, she seemed to be more experienced and mature.

"I love you," I said, in a moment of pure passion, while my finger was rubbing her clitoris.

She laughed and made me feel foolish, but I knew I meant it. Her skin was so soft, and her tongue so inquisitive that I was in a state of bliss. I would have said or believed anything to prolong the moment. Young love is so wonderful at first. Your mind and heart race into a state of unreality, which is impenetrable to reasoning. She was a challenge, not because she wouldn't touch me, but because she kept her emotions in control and wouldn't give away her heart right then. She was playing, having fun, and she wanted to be in charge, while I capitulated and fell right into her trap.

I clung to the "not yet," intimating perhaps that one day she would be mine, heart and soul, to do with her as I wished. After we sweated through two hours of petting, we walked quickly out of the apartment and went to sit in a nearby park. Children were playing loudly, while the parents chatted and screamed at their kids. The cities in Italy are so alive; people speak more quickly, as if every moment is urgent, but they might sit in same spot for hours. They don't work like we do, silently and stoically for long hours. They are a culture of spirit and mind; the day revolves around the excitement of interaction. Kristen enjoyed watching people, as did I, and we just sat and talked, soaking up the environs.

"What do you write about?" I asked.

"The beauty of life and nature," she said.

"May I read some of your work sometime?" I said.

"Sure."

"Do you ever write about the ugly or depressing side of life, or the destructiveness of nature?" I said.

"Sometimes, but usually to set off or contrast it with beauty."

"That's interesting," I said. "I take it you are an optimist."

"I guess so, but I don't think of myself in those terms," she said.

"Really, I thought most people considered themselves either optimists or pessimists."

"I have too great a range of thoughts and emotions to label them so simply," she said. "I think of myself as a Romantic."

"You remind me of Virginia Woolf."

"Funny you should mention that," she said. "There's something I have to tell you."

"Go ahead," I said.

"I like women as much as men."

It took a second for that to sink in, but when I realized what she meant, it didn't bother me.

"You've had affairs with women?" I asked.

"Just twice, but they were very intense, more intense than the men I've been with."

"It's difficult enough competing with other men, but add women and I feel outnumbered," I said.

"Don't be threatened," she said. "I like you. I only go out with one person at a time, and I expect it'll be you as long as things work out," she said.

"That's somewhat reassuring, but it might take some time for me to get used to the idea," I said. "In fact, the more I think about it, the less I like it."

"I thought you might react that way, but I had to be honest," she said.

We were silent for a long time, and I thought perhaps it was a good thing she had told me her secret. If I were in her position, I might not have said anything. I probably would have kept it a secret, until I had become more involved. The thing is, I still liked her. I imagined her making love to another woman and had mixed emotions. The thought was sexually exciting, but I was also horrified by the image. Being heterosexual, I didn't understand bisexuality. I must admit it threatened me, hitting so close to home. I didn't know what to think about it; I was baffled.

"Why do you think people are gay, bisexual, or straight?" I asked her.

"I have no idea," she said.

"You said your experiences with women were more intense than with men. Maybe you're gay and not bisexual," I observed.

"I don't know that either," she said. "If it bothers you that much, maybe we shouldn't go out."

"Maybe we should cool it and get to know each other better," I said.

"That's a good idea," she assented.

Pigeons were walking about picking at crumbs on the sidewalk, not bothered by the noise on the street. I felt better that we had decided to relax and get to discover more about each other. She had a furrowed brow and seemed disturbed by her feelings and thoughts. On the other hand, I still felt the excitement of being in Florence; I couldn't get enough of looking at the architecture and the trees. I loved to watch the Italians, who reminded me so much of my father and my cousins who still lived in Rome. Although I wanted to say something loving to Kristen, to dispel her troubling thoughts, I didn't know what to say.

"This is going to be a great year," I said.

"Yes, it is," she said.

"Well, listen, I've got some reading to do, so I'll see you tomorrow in school," I said.

"Yeah, I've got some work to do as well," she said.

It felt uncomfortable parting with her, but I wanted to be alone for a while to sort out my thoughts. I walked back to my room and relaxed, reading some of my assignments, but I was really thinking about Kristen the whole time.

Chapter Five

Dinner was very important at our household. My Italian "mother" spent the entire day in the kitchen, making jams and canning vegetables, as well as preparing for the evening meal. We were all assembled to eat at about seven o'clock, and the table was always lively with conversation. Sergio and Riccardo wanted to hear about the States. They had never traveled there and had only seen photographs, mostly of New York City. They wanted to hear about the women, because they said they always had difficulty dating them. I told them some funny stories about American women, and added that Italian women were some of the most sought after in the world. We ate well, with a glass of Chianti, and solved all the world's problems.

After dinner, I called Horace and asked him if he could get away for the evening. He said he could, so we met at the school, just as the sun was setting over the orange tiled roofs of the city. Horace brought a bottle of vodka with him, and we started drinking it out of a brown paper bag as we walked through the city.

"Does Melanie mind if you go out by yourself?" I asked.

"She does, but she doesn't say anything," he said.

Horace was more of a drinker than I, and he could hold his liquor better. I started feeling the effects of the vodka almost immediately. The narrow streets of downtown seemed even narrower, and I found myself giggling at everything Horace said. We were looking for adventure, and it wasn't long before we found it. A man was walking down the street, and I asked him where we could find some prostitutes. He directed me to a park on the West side of town. I didn't want to have anything to do with a whore, but Horace was intent on finding one.

"Why do you want a whore? Doesn't Melanie satisfy you?" I said.

"She won't give me blow jobs; I have to go hunting for those," he said.

We found the park, after asking for directions again, but we didn't see anybody hanging around.

"Be patient," Horace said.

The park lights reflected off the trees, making the atmosphere romantic, giving me pause as to why we were there. Horace lit a cigarette and leaned against a lamppost, looking a little like Humphrey Bogart. I was getting pretty drunk, and the shadows seemed to be moving. We must have been waiting for only ten minutes when a woman came walking by. Horace waved to her, and she came over to us. He wanted me to translate, but I didn't know how to say blowjob in Italian, and I was laughing again. Horace just said "Quanto?" and gestured with his hand. The woman gave him a price, and they disappeared into the bushes. Five minutes later, they emerged, and she walked off with a look of dignity. I was laughing so hard when he told me he hadn't even come.

As we walked through the city, Horace told me stories of Georgia. It was a world I wasn't familiar with. They used to get in fights every Friday night at the American Legion, and Horace would team up with his brothers until they won or lost. His father had built a shack out of odd pieces of wood, on a seven-acre lot, where they farmed most of their land. He was the eldest of seven children and had a great deal of responsibility growing up, as his mother had disappeared. They used to go hunting and trapping and did a great deal of fishing in the summer.

I found out that Horace had got into drugs pretty heavily in the seventies and had supported himself for a few years by dealing pot. Even though by description, Horace sounds like a detestable person, he was very fun loving and very likeable. Whenever he was around, the world seemed exciting. He told me some things I wouldn't even repeat, but for the most part, I knew he exaggerated his stories and even made them up altogether to keep the conversation lively.

Horace and I split up after a few hours of walking through the city. I was pretty drunk, and I wanted to see Kristen. It was about eleven thirty, and I thought she might still be awake. When I arrived at her apartment building, I discovered that it was locked. I was thinking of shouting up to her window, but the city was so quiet. I thought I might get arrested. I noticed there was a tree next to the building that stretched out over her window. With some effort, I climbed the tree, almost falling out of it at one point, but when I reached her window, I didn't know what to do. At first, I called her name softly, then more loudly, but there was no response. Next I broke a twig off the tree and tossed it at the window. No response. I tried it a few more times, until finally, she turned on her light and came to the window.

"What the hell are you doing?" she said.

"I have to see you!" I said.

"You're drunk," she said.

"A little," I said.

"Go home and sleep it off. I'm not coming out," she said.

"You don't understand, Kristen. I love you!" I slurred.

"You're crazy. Go home, Paul," she said, as she closed the

shutters.

I started to climb down the tree, but before I could get half way, I threw up all over myself. I was too drunk to care, but when I reached my apartment, I made sure I was perfectly quiet going to my room. I was just about to climb into bed, when I realized I had better go to the bathroom to get cleaned up. Sergio was coming out of the bathroom as I got there, and he just stared at me in shock as I walked past him.

The next morning, hung over, I crawled out of bed and shuffled to the kitchen for my cappuccino. The whole family was having breakfast, but nobody said a word to me. I realized immediately that my behavior was unacceptable, and I apologized to the Signora for my late arrival the night before. Then I remembered climbing the tree at Kristen's place, and felt like a jerk.

I dragged myself to school and found Horace sitting in the café, chatting just as brightly as ever. He looked at me and just laughed.

"How ya feeling, Paul? You look a little worse for wear," he joked.

"I'll never do that again," I mumbled.

"Oh, it's good for you; builds character," he said.

Little did I know then that ten years later I would smoke pot every day – all day! I didn't like alcohol much, but I drank some wine most evenings that year in Italy. I didn't have a problem then, but I was building the groundwork for a problem later on. Horace was already a full-blown alcoholic, but he seemed to handle it relatively well. He didn't drink all day when he was in Florence, only in the evenings, but usually just a few glasses of wine, not a bottle of vodka like he did in the States.

"That kind of character I don't need," I said.

Kristen walked in and gave me a shaming look. Feeling foolish, I just smiled at her. Monica was sitting with Ellen, and they seemed involved in a heavy conversation. I sat next to Horace and sipped my coffee slowly, thinking that I would go home and sleep some more. Jesse came in a few minutes later and sat down with us.

"Hey, Paul, John and I are looking at an apartment, and we need a third, are you interested?"

"Sure, how much is it?" I said.

"It's about two hundred apiece, which is cheaper than what we're paying to stay with the families," he said.

After our classes, John, Jesse, and I went to look at the apartment. It was on the other side of the river, and we had a view of the hills west of the city. It was a beautiful space, and we decided immediately to take it. We flipped a coin to see who would have their own room, and I won. John and Jesse were perfectly happy sharing a room, but I was planning on entertaining women, so I was glad I had some privacy.

The space was very simple, a living room, a small kitchen, and two large bedrooms. It was sparsely furnished, but we didn't need much. Both bedrooms had a nice view, and there was a beautiful garden below our windows. We had to give our families a couple of weeks notice. There was no yearly contract; we were free to move rather quickly. My Italian "brothers" were upset that I was moving out, but I promised them I would visit often.

For the next two weeks, I behaved myself and went to bed at a normal hour, making sure not to disturb the Signora. I had coffee or lunch with Kristen almost every day, but we kept to ourselves in the evenings. Much of the time, I found myself fantasizing about Monica, but I was afraid to ask her out. I would talk to her in school, and we became closer, but there was a line that I wouldn't dare cross yet.

When we moved into our apartment, everything changed. Since it was the only apartment in the group, it became the center of our social circle. Horace and Melanie came over for dinner almost every night, bringing a big bottle of Chianti, and Horace did most of the cooking. George, an artist friend of ours, hung out during the day, and life in Florence became one long social hour.

Kristen and I became just friends. The initial infatuation wore off, and I started dating a young woman named Laura. Laura was three-quarters Italian, and a quarter Irish. She was lively, argumentative, funny, and very sexy. She had long brown hair pulled back in a ponytail, large brown eyes with long lashes, and delicately arched eyebrows. She said she had been watching me closely since we had departed New York, and was just biding her time until she made her move.

Laura started coming over to our apartment the very week we moved in. She often brought flowers, vegetables, and cheeses from the open market downtown. On warm days she wore short, colorful skirts that showed off her slender legs. It was great to have her come over. She brightened the atmosphere with her vitality.

At first, we thought she was interested in John, but one day she came into my room while I was reading on my bed, and she lay down next to me. I was pleasantly surprised and didn't hesitate to grab her and start mauling her. She kissed me so forcefully that I had a hard time breathing. It wasn't long before I tore her clothes off and began licking her all over.

"I want to suck your cock," she whispered to me.

"Feel free!" I exclaimed, as I pulled my pants off.

"You taste so good," she said.

It took me a long time to lick her pussy and make her come, but finally I gave her an orgasm. She screamed in delight, and I worried that my roommates had heard her.

"I want you inside me," she said.

I thrust my cock in her so hard, I thought I hurt her, but she assured me it was okay. Then I told her to roll over, and I pushed up against her plump ass.

"Fuck me in the ass," she said.

I couldn't believe my ears. I had never heard a woman say that before. At first I hesitated, then decided to try it. Her ass was so tight I couldn't penetrate her, so I grabbed some Vaseline and eased it inside her.

"Oh," she moaned, "that feels great!"

After thrusting it in her ass for just a couple of minutes, I came and came. I had never been so excited in my life. I was so excited that I felt like telling her I loved her, but I restrained myself. We were exhausted but felt satisfied. I had no idea where this relationship was going, but I know I liked her and besides, I wasn't willing to think beyond that point.

We lay there together, staring at the ceiling, talking intimately for the first time.

"I liked you the minute I saw you in New York," she said.

"How can you like somebody without even talking to them?" I said.

"I don't know. I liked your features. You seemed intelligent and sensitive. Then I was pleased to discover you had a sense of humor," she said.

"I like your vivaciousness," I said.

She rolled over and leaned on her elbow, and I gently

rubbed her ass, talking as if we had been married for years. Her delicate hand was placed on my hip. She was perfectly relaxed and so was I.

"You have quite a bit of experience in bed," I said.

"I had a boyfriend for a few years, and we tried all kinds of things," she said.

"I was shocked when you said, 'Fuck me in the ass'; I've never done that before," I said.

"I hesitated to say it, but my boyfriend and I used to do it all the time," she said.

"I liked it," I said.

Laura lit a cigarette and got up from the bed, her slender body attracting my stare. She strode to the window and looked out over the landscape.

"I wish I were in an apartment," she said.

"Maybe you and a couple of the gals could get a place," I said.

"I'll ask around," she said.

We talked for a long time, sharing stories of our childhoods and our family backgrounds. She was from a wealthy family and was attending Brown University. She was a painter and a sculptor and had been an athlete in high school. Laura was sure of herself, but she didn't seem arrogant or self-centered. She told me that her father was very strict, while her mother was gentle and understanding. Her father had a temper, like so many Italian men, but she loved him dearly, and they got along pretty well. I told her my father had a temper too, but that we loved each other.

"My mother is a teacher, and she's great. She's patient and tolerant," I said. "My parents were divorced. Both of them remarried, but I think my mother might get divorced again," I said.

"Sounds like she picks men that are difficult to get along with," Laura observed.

"She picks very intelligent men, but that doesn't mean they are emotionally mature," I said.

"Listen," she said, "I know you have your eye on some of the other women."

"No," I started to say.

"Let me finish," she said.

"I don't expect you to go out with only me. If you want to date other women, that's fine."

"I've never heard a woman say that," I said, "but I'm really a one woman at a time guy."

"Good," she said.

Chapter Six

John, Jesse, and I became very close. We spent most of our time together playing cards, especially in the afternoon. In the evenings, Horace and Melanie came over for dinner, and Laura showed up regularly. We were like a family. We stuck together since we didn't have families there. Sometimes Laura would sketch me in the nude. Her drawings were excellent, and after the work, we would make love.

John began dating a woman named Patricia, and she quickly became a member of our extended family. She was tall and slender with big blue eyes and dirty blonde hair, which she usually pulled back. She had a great sense of humor and became best friends with Laura. Jesse was not much of a ladies' man, and spent the whole year not really dating anyone, even though we often encouraged him to take the plunge.

Laura and I began visiting museums in the afternoons; we exchanged opinions on most of the pieces, and I discovered she was much more informed than I was. In the evening, we usually made love, but it was not as frenetic as the first time. As we got to know each other, we would spend an hour on tender foreplay, and then have intercourse for another half hour. We both enjoyed oral sex. I would make her come two or three times just by licking her, and she would suck me for a long time before I entered her.

We were quickly becoming known as a couple, and I noticed most of the other women staying away from me.

Monica remained my friend. Our rapport didn't change at all. She talked to me in the café every morning, and I noticed at these times that Laura would pretend not to be jealous.

Even though I spent most of my time with Laura, I thought about Monica a great deal. Because Monica and I were just friends, we were able to open up and share intimate thoughts. One afternoon I posed for Monica, although not in the nude, and we talked for two hours about all our deepest secrets. She shared with me that she had kissed a woman for a long time when she was fourteen, and had been fearful that she was gay. I was thinking of telling her about Kristen, but I didn't. It had been shared with me privately, and I knew I had no business talking about it.

"Are you seeing anyone now?" I asked Monica.

"I'm spending some time with an Italian guy, but I wouldn't call it dating. He's a banker in his early thirties. I think he's too old for me, but we have fun," she said.

"Why don't you go out with me?" I said, before I could stop myself.

"Aren't you pretty serious with Laura?" she said.

"Sort of, but I find myself thinking about you much of the time," I said.

"We can spend time together like we are now," she said, "but I don't want to get serious with you."

"Why not?"

She didn't answer. I guess it was understood that it was simply a matter of feelings. I looked out over the rooftops, through the window behind her and laughed to myself.

I always wanted the one I couldn't have, and the one I had wasn't good enough. I thought about Laura, as I gazed out the window, and I decided she was good enough. She was just as nice as Monica, just as good looking, and she was great in bed. But there was something about Monica.

The painting didn't turn out great, but it was decent. Her colors were interesting, subtle hues of brown and deep, dark maroon highlighted by deep greens and yellows. She used white sparingly. The painting was definitely dark, but interesting. I never thought then that someday I would pick up a paintbrush myself and learn to paint.

"It needs work," she said.

"I like it," I said.

I asked her if I could keep it, and she agreed. I took it home to show the boys, and they teased me about posing fully clothed. John and Jesse were not artists, but they appreciated the effort. Laura popped in later in the afternoon and was visibly jealous of the painting.

"It's good," she said.

"You could probably do better," I said.

"Why don't you pose for me?" she said.

"In the nude?" I said.

"Of course," she said.

"I will, soon," I said.

Before dinner, Laura and I walked along the river, talking intimately.

"Do you like Monica?" she asked me.

"We're just friends," I said.

"But do you like her?"

"Yes," I said, though as soon as I said it, I wished I hadn't.

"Why don't you go out with her?" she said.

"She doesn't like me that way," I said.

She was silent for a minute, probably contemplating how

dangerous it was that Monica was indifferent toward me.

"Are you trying to get rid of me?" I said.

"No," she said.

"Let's change the subject," I said.

"Tell me what you want to write about," she said.

"I don't really know," I said, "I guess about what's important."

"Lots of things are important. What do you know about?"

"Nothing, it seems," I said.

"You should focus on your own life," she said. "The more intimately, the better."

"My life doesn't seem particularly extraordinary," I said.

"That's why so many people will identify with it," she said.

"Do you think identification is so key?" I said.

"Absolutely, people want to read about things they understand and see every day, about themselves and how they compare to you."

"It seems to me most people read about things that don't relate to them at all," I said.

"Well, you're not going to write mysteries or science fiction, are you?"

"No, or course not," I said.

"Who do you like to read?" she asked.

"I like Hardy, Lawrence, Proust, Conrad, all the moderns really."

"Yeah, I like them, too," she said.

The traffic was busy along the river; Italians drive insanely, and it was pretty bad, so we turned down a narrow side street. The sky was a dark blue, etched between the tiled roofs. I thought about writing and wondered what I would write about someday. I liked talking about relationships and thought that maybe I would write about people mostly. Also, I liked philosophy and wanted to include some discussion of ideas. Beyond that, I knew nothing.

"Write about me," she said.

"Maybe I will," I said. "Should I include our private experiences?"

"Sure! That's what makes it juicy," she said.

We turned back after a while and went home to eat dinner. Dinner was always festive. We felt like Italians, drinking wine, talking loudly. It was a great way to end the day. Life was more exciting in Florence; I would rarely feel such elation at home, and I thought maybe someday I would move to Italy permanently.

Chapter Seven

Laura attacked me that night. She liked to experiment in bed, as if lovemaking were an adventure. She licked my anus for the first time, a sensation I'll never forget, and something that many women would never attempt. We laughed in bed and felt like kids playing a game. I didn't know if I was in love, but I sure enjoyed making love to her. When Laura and I were in bed, I never thought about Monica. We spent a great deal of time lying naked next to each other, touching and talking. She told me about her long-term boyfriend, and all the tricks they used to perform in bed. She really enjoyed sucking my cock, but she would tease me, bringing me to the brink of orgasm, and then she would stop for a while before resuming. I loved coming in her mouth and watching her swallow it.

"Do you like this?" she said, sticking her finger up my ass.

"Gently," I said. "Do you have an obsession with asses?" I asked.

"Not really. Why?" she said, sounding slightly offended.

"I don't know. That's one area I never touched before," I said.

"You like it, don't you?" she said.

"I must admit I do. It was always taboo before," I said.

I thought about D.H. Lawrence, who had written about that taboo, and about a lively conversation we had in class one day talking about it. However, it was not the same thing as doing it. After making love, Laura went to Jesse's room to bum a couple of cigarettes. We didn't smoke, but we thought we would have one after sex to see if it was as good as they said. I coughed violently after my first puff, but I managed to finish the cigarette.

Laura laughed at me and held her cigarette like a movie star, blowing smoke rings into the air. We had fun. There was no doubt about it, but as soon as she left, I started thinking about Monica. I called her on the phone, but she was out, and wondered who she was out with. I went to sleep feeling great and excited about the coming day.

I woke up before dawn and decided to go out for a walk with my camera to catch the city as the sun was rising. I walked across our bridge and took one of my best photographs of the Ponte Vecchio reflected in the river. Next, I walked through the nearly deserted streets of downtown and marveled at the city. At one point I came upon the statue of David, one of the many replicas scattered around Florence. As streaks of sun flooded the morning sky, I stared at David's face, and got a rush of adrenaline. I too would slay Goliath, the giant of writing, attacking the paper as so many had done before me. I didn't know how difficult it would be; I would not be surrounded by people encouraging me or offering applause. My desire would eventually come from the love of writing alone. Like self-love, it has to be generated every day by beauty or ugliness, by hate, love, or fear, or by whatever might spark my interest at that moment.

The writer is a Renaissance man, whether he or she picks up any other art. The whole world is available to the writer, and he or she must conquer it. First, I would have to study all the classic writers. What were their subjects and concerns, and how is our time different?

"What is significant about my life?" I wondered to myself.

I walked home feeling elated, as though I had already written my first book.

Shortly after that, I got to school early and chatted with Aldo, who served my coffee. He was an older man, possessing the typical Italian sense of humor. Not long after I arrived, Horace walked in with Melanie. He pulled me aside and whispered in my ear: "She gave me a blow job last night!" His eyes were sparkling.

"It must be Italy," I said.

"This place is unbelievable," he said happily.

The three of us sat down and chatted about people in the program, our favorite topic. When Melanie was refilling her cappuccino, I told Horace about my lovemaking the night before.

"God, I wish I wasn't married!" he said.

"Do you guys want to come over for dinner tonight?" I asked.

"Sure," Horace said. "I'll cook."

A few minutes later, Monica walked in and smiled at us as she ordered her coffee. I stepped up to the counter next to her and talked to her for a minute before asking her to dinner. She accepted graciously, but right away I wondered if I had done something wrong. Laura would certainly be coming over too, and I thought there might be a conflict.

I went shopping for food in the afternoon at the downtown market. It was a lively scene of people and wonderful scents. I bought some vegetables, cheeses, meats, and wine and walked a mile home with my heavy bags.

The thought of dinner was making me nervous. I didn't

know how Laura would react to having Monica around, but I thought she would probably handle it well. Laura was not the jealous type, but her talk of an open relationship was really a lot of bullshit. Horace and Melanie showed up at five, and he put me right to work, prepping the food. Monica came about half an hour later with a camera and started taking pictures of us cooking. John and Patricia helped set the table and kept the wine flowing. Jesse kept Melanie company while Horace cooked. Laura showed up about six and didn't seem at all upset about seeing Monica.

We sat down to a veritable banquet of fish and chicken, sausages, broccoli, carrots, potatoes, and various cheeses, but we were Americans after all, so we ate as much as we could.

"This chicken is great," John said. "How did you make it?"

"It's a secret recipe handed down through generations," Horace said.

Laura rubbed her foot against mine, while I tried to engage Monica in conversation.

"Will you do another painting of me?" I asked Monica.

"Sure, but I hope the next one turns out better," she said.

"I thought you were going to sit for me?" Laura said.

"I will," I said. "I can sit for both of you."

"Now that sounds interesting," Horace said, "but I really think you should be naked." He laughed.

"Nude is the word," Monica said.

"Naked, nude, what's the difference?" Horace said. "All I want to know is if Paul is posing nude and you're painting his cock. What happens if all of a sudden it gets hard?"

"Spritz a little cold water on it," Laura said.

"You might need a bucket!" Horace said.

We laughed the rest of the night, and I was careful to give

more attention to Laura than Monica. Horace was the life of the party. I noticed he drank a lot more than the others and never stopped talking or laughing. Jesse seemed quiet. I think he had trouble opening up in a group. After the party, I talked to him for a little while. John and Patricia went to bed, while Jesse and I cleaned up. Laura decided to leave. She didn't want to get in the habit of spending every night with me. Monica was pretty drunk when she left, but refused to have anyone walk her home.

Chapter Eight

At about ten o'clock that evening, I called Monica to see that she made it home all right. She only had a few blocks to walk, but it was a good excuse for me to call her.

"How are you feeling?" I said.

"I'm pretty sober now; I had three cups of coffee," she said.

"I didn't realize you could drink so much," I said.

"I only had four glasses of wine, but I'm not used to it. How many did you have?" she said.

"I didn't keep track, but I caught a buzz that's for sure," I said.

"Horace sure can drink, can't he?" she said.

"Yeah, he's a professional," I said.

I wanted to get into a more intimate conversation, but I was afraid to say anything too personal. She knew I was interested in her but was aloof and didn't show any emotion. I imagined her in her nightgown with her makeup washed off, getting ready for bed.

"What do you think of Horace and Melanie?" I said.

"An odd couple to be sure. Do you know how they met?" she asked.

"They worked at the same restaurant. Horace was the manager and Melanie was a waitress, working part-time while she went to Duke," I said.

"I've never seen such a disparity between classes of people," she said.

"Well, I guess we don't really live in a classless society, do we?" I said.

"Hardly," she said.

"He's exceptional though; you know it. Even though he has a high school degree, he really knows a great deal. He studies with her every night. He's interested in everything," I said.

"He winked at me tonight," she said.

"So?" I said.

"Well, it was in a lustful way. I don't think he's perfectly faithful," she said.

"He did tell me he cheated a couple of times, but he says he really loves Melanie," I said.

"Convenient," she said.

"Do you want to have lunch with me tomorrow?" I said.

There was a long pause. I didn't like the fact that she had to think about it.

"Sure, but it can't be until two; I have studio until then," she said.

"Oh, great! Well, I'll talk to you tomorrow," I said.

"Bye," she said.

I was excited all of a sudden, as if I had made a breakthrough with her. I was so thrilled about having lunch with her that I didn't fall asleep for two hours. I kept imagining my first kiss with her, and then slipping my hand up her skirt, then down her pants. I also imagined her slapping my face and rudely turning me out of her apartment. I felt guilty about Laura, but not enough to keep me from chasing Monica. Finally, I fell asleep. When I woke up, I felt hung over.

I could hardly pay attention in class the next day, because I kept thinking about lunch. I knew it didn't mean so much to Monica, but I fantasized that somehow this would be the beginning of a more serious turn in our relationship. Laura wanted to have lunch with me too, but I made some excuse. My life was becoming more complicated every day, but at that point it was still under control.

I met Monica in the café after her class and took her to a nearby trattoria, which we had heard was very good. Not too many people were in the restaurant, so we had three waiters taking care of us. The pasta was delicious, and I got a sensuous pleasure out of watching Monica eat.

"You seem pretty tired after last night," she said.

"Yes, I'm going to take a nap as soon as I get home," I said.

"I'm tired too, and I didn't get much painting done this morning," she said.

"What are you working on?" I said.

"I'm working on a landscape from a photograph; it's an assignment for class, and it's really difficult."

"Which is more difficult, a figure or a landscape?" I said.

"For me a figure is much more difficult, especially a realistic rendition."

"I can see why," I said.

There were pauses in our conversation as we ate our food, and I kept thinking that I wanted our talk to become more serious. At one point I ventured out into vulnerable territory.

"Monica, I think we should go out, you know, date on a regular basis," I said.

"Umm, I don't think so, Paul," she said.

"Why not?"

"I've been watching you these weeks, and you're constantly changing from one girlfriend to another. I just wonder who will be after me, Ellen maybe?"

"No, that's not the way it is at all. I really care for you. I don't want to go out with anyone else. The reason I've switched around is because none of them measure up to you."

"I'm sure," she said.

I became very frustrated and almost angry with her for judging me that way. She had me cornered, and I knew I wouldn't be able to change her mind.

"You're just going to leave Laura for no reason at all?" she asked.

I didn't know what to say to that, and I took a bite of pasta and looked at my plate. Then a thought came to me. What if Monica told Laura what I had said?

"You wouldn't tell Laura any of this, would you?" I said.

"No, of course not," she said.

I changed the subject and we ate the rest of the meal, making polite conversation. Even though she had flatly rejected me, I wasn't about to give up. I thrived on rejection. It only made the challenge that much greater. After lunch, we parted ways. She went back to school, and I went home. Jesse and John were playing cards when I arrived, so I joined them and told them what had transpired with Monica.

Chapter Nine

Horace came over for dinner alone. Melanie was busy studying, and he wanted to go out on the town that evening. He cooked a fancy pasta dish that he had read about, with shrimp and scallops. It was a delicious meal, and Horace encouraged me to forget about Monica, which I couldn't do. We drank quite a bit of wine and laughed about everything. Horace told more stories about the Deep South, and he made it sound as though every minute had been an adventure.

At about nine o'clock, we went out looking for fun, and I was hoping we wouldn't get into any trouble.

"Are you trying to find another whore?" I asked him.

"We'll see. Not particularly. I just want to see what happens in this town at night," he said.

We walked toward the outskirts of town, through very quiet neighborhoods. There was not one part of town that contained many bars or nightclubs. They were hidden in different areas. As we were walking and sipping wine, we happened upon an opium den that was located in the basement of a building.

It was a very strange place with all kinds of people walking from room to room, smoking various things and not talking very much. I had an eerie feeling as soon as I strolled in, but Horace was fascinated. He spotted a young woman sitting in a corner, holding a pipe, and sat down next to her. She looked like she was in another world. I sat next to Horace and told him I wanted to leave. He said we would just stay a little while.

Without speaking a word of Italian, he made it clear to the young woman that he wanted to share the pipe, and he gave her some money.

"Do you know what you're smoking?" I asked Horace.

"It's got to give you a hell of a buzz, whatever it is," he said.

"I've never smelled anything like it," I said.

"I think it's opium," he said.

A few seconds later, Horace was flying high. He stopped talking to me and concentrated on the girl. In a few minutes Horace was sticking his hand down her pants. I told him I wanted to leave, again, but he paid no attention to me. I decided I would just go and let him do what he wanted. I had the greatest feeling walking out into the fresh air, and I tried to find my bearings, so that I could take the shortest route home. I felt a little guilty about leaving him behind, but I figured he could take care of himself.

For a little while, I was lost, but then I happened upon a main street that I was familiar with. As I was walking, it began to rain. I had no jacket and no hat. Before long, I was soaking wet. I began to feel sorry for myself, which led to thoughts of Monica, and soon I was miserable. I wished I had played it like John, not getting involved too quickly and picking the best one for the whole year. I didn't know why Laura didn't interest me too much, and the more I thought about it, the less apparent it became.

It was rather late when I arrived home, and I immediately took a warm bath, which made me feel better. It occurred to me that Horace might be angry, but there was nothing I could do about it now.

John was still awake, apparently, because I heard him walking around while I was in the tub. After my bath, we talked for a little while.

"Did you have a good time?" he said.

"Not at all. We found this eerie opium den, and it was the spookiest place I have every seen. Horace might still be there for all I know."

"He's a wild one," John said.

"Yeah, I don't think I want to hang out with him at night. I love it when he comes over for dinner and cooks, but after that he tends to look for trouble," I said.

"He's not in school, so he can stay out as late as he wants and sleep in during the day, but you've got to get up early," he said.

"You're right," I said.

"You seem kind of down," he said.

"Yes, I think it's because I'm obsessed with Monica, and she's not interested," I said.

"That's hard. I've been there," he said.

"What kills me is that I should be in love with Laura; she's a great woman, but I'm just not!"

"Cheer up. Things will work out. There are plenty of women around," he said.

"I guess you're right."

I was glad to go to bed. I was really exhausted, but I knew I would have trouble getting up in the morning. I kept thinking about leaving Horace in that horrible place, but there was nothing I could do about it now. Even though I was fatigued, it took me a long time to fall asleep. In the morning, sure enough, I felt hung over, but decided I would still get up on time and go to school. I took some aspirin and felt better after an hour.

I walked to school through the Piazza della Signora and stared at the replica of the David for a minute. I didn't feel all that heroic that morning, and my interpretation of his stern face was that of perseverance during difficult times. It occurred to me then that each time I passed him, I would have a new interpretation. The streets were busy and loud. I loved the activity of a bustling city.

When I got to school, Horace was sitting in the café with a big grin on his face. I couldn't help but laugh. Laura was sitting with him, but Melanie was in class. I ordered a double cappuccino and plunked myself down next to them.

"That was a strange place, huh, Paulie?" Horace said.

"How long did you stay?" I asked.

"I left about half an hour after you," he said.

"What kind of a place was it?" asked Laura.

"Some drug-filled den; it was downstairs, and one of the strangest places I've ever been in," I said.

Monica walked in after a few minutes, and I think Laura noticed me watching her. Monica moved so gracefully, like a dancer. She had a silk skirt on, light green, and I could see the outlines of her ass through it. Monica waved to us, but left us as soon as she got her coffee. Laura didn't say anything, but I knew she was jealous.

"Did you have a good time, Horace?" Laura said.

"Not really, but it was different," he laughed.

A few minutes later, it was time for class, so Laura and I left Horace by himself. As I sat listening about the genius of DaVinci, my mind wandered to Monica's ass, wiggling gently behind her silk skirt. The art of life for me at the time was appreciating beautiful women, and I couldn't get enough of them. Monica was elusive, and the challenge captivated me.

Perhaps if she had given in right away, she would have no longer interested me. I didn't want to settle down; I wanted to conquer.

After classes, Laura and I went out to lunch. She talked throughout the meal, while I thought about how to get out of the relationship. I know it sounds callous, but I was young, and I couldn't appreciate what I had. Thinking that I would break up with her that night, I invited her over for dinner. I spent the rest of the afternoon rehearsing my speech, trying to let her down as easily as possible. I thought of several lines to tell her, but just decided to admit that I didn't love her.

While I was making dinner, I was very nervous, and she realized something was up.

"What's the matter, Paul?" she said, noticing a difference in my manner.

"Nothing," I said.

"Are you sure?"

"I'm fine," I said.

Actually, I was all confused. She was wearing a pair of tight jeans, and a tiny tank top that was driving me crazy. I thought I would put off the speech for another night. After dinner, we were talking on my bed about nothing in particular, and all I could think about was sex. I waited for the right moment and kissed her. She responded immediately. She wanted to take her clothes off right away, but I wanted to peel them off one item at a time. She was delicious.

I pulled her top up to her neck and slowly sucked on her nipples. She started groaning and pressed her breasts against me. It entered my mind that I was being a hypocrite, but I wasn't going to stop now. She unbuttoned my shirt and kissed the length of my body. I was already hard, and she fumbled with my pants for a few seconds before my cock popped out. She started licking slowly along the length of it before putting it in her mouth.

Suddenly, I thought about breaking up with her in the future, and my hard on disappeared.

"What's the matter?" she said.

"I don't know," I said. "I don't think I can do this."

She appeared very disappointed, and I knew she was blaming herself.

"It's not your fault," I said. "I've got a lot on my mind."

"You don't find me attractive any more," she said.

"I do. That's not it. It's just that I want to see other women," I said.

She started to cry and said:

"I knew this was coming."

"I didn't want to tell you like this. It just happened; I should have said something earlier," I said.

"It's all right. There's no good way to break up with somebody," she said.

I was very surprised that she wasn't angry. The other women I had broken up with were all angry. This was the first time somebody had reacted with overwhelming sadness. Her reaction made me feel sad too.

"We'll still be good friends," I said.

There was no appeasing her. She kept crying until she exhausted herself. I wanted to hold her in my arms, but something kept me from doing it. I knew her pain would go away eventually, and suddenly I had a feeling of freedom. Laura decided to leave, and I solemnly walked her to the door. Immediately, I wondered if I had made a mistake, but I decided I had been honest with myself.

Chapter Ten

When I went to school the next day, I felt like a boy in a candy store, because I was a free man, and there were many available women around. Ellen was sitting in the café studying, so I ordered a cappuccino and sat down with her. She was wearing tight jeans and a dark gray sweater that clung to her body. She had curled her brown hair and had put makeup on, which must have been for the first time all year.

"You look great, Ellen. You really fixed yourself up," I said.

"Every once in a while, when I'm feeling low, I put makeup on," she said.

"What's the matter?" I said.

"I just got a Dear Ellen letter from my boyfriend back home. He's found somebody else," she said.

She wasn't crying, but she had the most depressed look on her face. I reached out my hand and held hers for a second, and she smiled in return.

"How long had you been going out?" I asked.

"A couple of years," she said, "but I was hoping we'd get married."

"You're too young to get married," I said, thinking that now I might have the opportunity to go out with her.

"I know, but he's such a great guy," she said.

"There are lots of great men around, and you're an attractive woman. You'll have several handsome men in the future," I said.

I didn't seem to be cheering her up at all, but I knew she was grateful that I was trying. There was a replica of a Renoir on the wall, a little girl in a pink dress, and I kept looking at it, fascinated.

"Not to change the subject or anything, but think of the difference between the so serious Renaissance paintings and the light, Romantic, almost innocent paintings of the Impressionists," I said.

"Some of the Renaissance paintings are not so serious," she said.

"I can't think of any like this," I said.

"You're right for the most part," she agreed, "and thanks for changing the subject."

"Why don't we have lunch today. I'll do a better job of cheering you up," I said.

"No thanks. I really appreciate it, but I'm afraid I wouldn't be good company," she said.

"Laura and I broke up last night," I said.

"Why?" Ellen said, surprised.

"I wasn't in love," I said.

"It's Monica, isn't it?" she said.

"Is it so obvious?" I said.

"She's a great woman," she said.

I looked wistfully out the window; the terra cotta roofs were gleaming in the sunlight. People were busily walking to work, and even though I was sad about Monica, I was glad I was in Italy. Ellen and I talked for a while, until the café began filling up, and it was time for class. I spent the day thinking about which women I wanted to date next, and didn't pay attention to anything the professors said. At eleven, when I had a break, I went to Monica's studio and looked over her shoulder while she painted.

"Do you have certain colors that you use more often?" I asked.

"Yes, I usually use the primary colors, but I change the tones a lot. I always seem to get a different feel, even though I use the same colors."

She didn't mind me watching her paint, and I learned a lot by observing, which I would apply years later when I painted. Her hair was pulled back in a ponytail, and while I watched her paint, I fantasized about running my hand through her silky hair.

"I'm going to lunch in a little while," I said. "Would you like to join me?"

"No thanks, I need to keep working on this; I'll see you later this afternoon."

I left the studio as if I had been turned down for a date, knowing full well she couldn't pull herself away from her work. I decided to eat by myself and walked home to see what the guys were cooking. John was home. He seemed to always be home, and I told him about my problems with women. He laughed and said I had no problems, which actually made me feel better.

In the afternoon, I went back to school refreshed after a nap and a good meal. I loved the way the Italians lived, taking a long break in the middle of the day. It was a partly cloudy day, and as I walked, I watched the shadows of the clouds pass by. When I walked in Florence, I turned my head a great deal to look in the shops and alleys, never tiring of the city landscape. I was planning to take a weekend in Venice, but I wanted to go with a woman, and I didn't know whom to ask. I only had one class in the afternoon, so I could spend most of my time leisurely sitting in the café, talking to friends.

Horace was sitting in his usual spot when I got there. He was chatting with a woman named Mary. I figured Melanie was in class. I sat down with them and ordered my fourth cappuccino of the day, which was the main reason I was so wound up. Mary was very cute and petite, half Italian, with big brown eyes and beautiful teeth. She had a high-pitched laugh, which rang out distinctly, and a tight little body. She was very sexy to look at. Mary and I didn't know each other very well, and I figured this would be the opportunity to get acquainted. Horace was in his usual friendly mood. He was grinning from ear to ear. He loved flirting with the women.

"Paulie, what's going on?" he said.

"Nothing much. I had a nice nap and lunch. I have nothing to do for a couple of hours. Melanie and I are going home. Why don't you keep Mary company?" he said, winking at me.

After Horace left, Mary and I talked about our classes, which professors we preferred, and other small talk. She asked me about Laura, and I told her we had broken up, which seemed to interest her. She wanted to know what had gone wrong, but wasn't satisfied with my answer that I just didn't love Laura.

"How do you know you don't love her? You were only together for a few weeks," she said.

"I don't know. I didn't feel like my affection was growing. I guess I'm still immature; if I don't feel the strong infatuation after a while, I figure I'm not in love," I said.

I took a sip of my cappuccino and tried to read her face. She seemed to be empathetic and didn't comment right away. After we were silent for a minute, she said:

"I'm probably no more mature than you are, but I know it

takes time to build love; infatuation burns off very quickly. Laura seems like a very lovable person."

I began feeling guilty for breaking up with Laura, but I wasn't going to tell Mary about my feelings for Monica. The café was thinning out as the afternoon wore on. Mary and I got into such an intense conversation about love that we decided to skip class and keep talking. I asked her if I could walk her home, and she agreed.

As we walked, I couldn't help but think that I would like to go out with her. She was sharp and witty; she easily kept up with my conversation, and she didn't mind challenging me on specific points.

"Do you live with a family?" I asked.

"I live with two older women, and they're constantly asking me what I'm doing and where I'm going," she said.

"That's not so good," I said, thinking that it might be difficult to invite her over to the apartment.

"Would you like to come over for dinner sometime?" I said.

"Sure, what about tomorrow?" she said.

I was almost shocked that she had volunteered so easily, and I thought that going out with her wouldn't be difficult at all. In the evening, the old streetlamps were lit and the city took on a different feeling. The antiquity of the buildings became more pronounced, and the quickly moving lights of the cars flashed across the streets. After I dropped off Mary, I felt elated just being in this beautiful city. I stopped at the supermarket and bought some food and a bottle of wine. When I arrived at the apartment, I found Horace and Melanie already cooking, as John and Jesse were setting the table.

"Any luck with Mary?" Horace said immediately.

"Yes, she's coming over for dinner tomorrow night. I really like her," I said.

Jesse shook his head. He couldn't believe I always had dates and girlfriends.

John laughed and said:

"You'd better slow down. You're going to go through all the women before the semester is over!"

After dinner, I went right to bed, exhausted from the day. I thought about Mary as I fell asleep, and I slept soundly all night.

Chapter Eleven

In the morning, I walked past the statue of David and realized perhaps that he was looking proud. I felt proud myself, even though I hadn't accomplished anything in particular. Actually, I was excited about beginning a new relationship, and as I always did, I envisioned being married to Mary and having a slew of children. With every woman I met, I always imagined a lifelong future with that woman, and the various details of what that might involve. I thought Mary was a good woman, and I enjoyed our conversation immensely, but I still couldn't get Monica out of my mind.

The café was bustling when I arrived. Horace, like a king, was sitting in his usual spot. Ellen and Melanie were sitting with him, listening to him as he held court. He nodded to me without interrupting one of his stories, and I sat down to listen. It was an outlandish tale of drinking and sexual perversion, like many of his other stories, and even though we knew he was probably lying or exaggerating, we enjoyed it thoroughly. I wanted to talk to Ellen alone, but didn't get the opportunity. I was almost reluctant to go to class, because Horace was on a roll and making us crack up.

I sat next to Mary in our Italian literature class, but I didn't say much to her. The class was centered on early twentieth century novels, and I found it fascinating. After class, Mary and I chatted on our way back to the café, and I told her to come over early for dinner, so we could have a glass of wine.

That evening, Horace cooked the dinner as usual, and Mary was enjoying herself.

"I never get to have dinner with people my own age," Mary said. "You guys are lucky to have your own apartment."

Horace made enough pasta for an army, and John took an extra large helping. Jesse hadn't come home yet, and we were all wondering where he was. Halfway through the meal, Jesse walked in with a wide smile on his face.

"Where have you been?" Horace asked.

"I had a date!" Jesse said.

We were all shocked and began quizzing him.

"Who did you go out with?" I said.

"Nobody you know," he said.

"What do you mean nobody we know," John said. "We know everybody in the program!"

"She's not in the program," Jesse said.

"She's Italian?" Horace said.

"German," Jesse said.

"German? Hey, that's great," John said. "Where did you meet her?"

"At a museum," Jesse said.

"What's she like?" I said.

"She's blonde and blue eyed of course, very intelligent, funny, and very nice," he said.

"Perfect!" Horace said.

Jesse sat down with a contented smile on his face and ate some pasta. Mary participated in the conversation like she was an old friend, and I was looking forward to being alone with her after dinner. Mary and I had a few glasses of wine with dinner and flirted the whole time. We played some cards after dinner and drank more wine. After cards, Mary and I excused ourselves and went into my room. I didn't hesitate a moment. I kissed her as soon as we sat on the bed, and the next minute we were groping each other with fervor.

Suddenly, she stopped me, as I was sliding my hand down her pants, and said:

"Slow down, Paul."

I went back to kissing her and sucking on her tits, rubbing my leg against her crotch. She was breathing very heavily, and I rubbed her cunt from the outside of her pants. I tried putting my hand down her pants again, and she got angry.

"Cut it out, Paul. I told you to stop and you keep pushing. I'm going home!"

"Don't go home. I'll stop; I promise," I said.

"You're just trying to fuck me. You don't want to develop any kind of relationship. I'm leaving," she said.

She dressed herself and left without saying another word, though I heard her politely saying goodbye to the others, who were in the living room. I felt bad, but I figured she'd feel better in a day or two. Then I figured Monica would somehow hear about it, making it even more difficult to get together with her.

I walked out to the living room looking a little sheepish, and the others just looked at me without saying anything. Finally, Horace said:

"You blew it, didn't you?"

I nodded my head and smiled, while Horace laughed.

"I went too fast for her," I said.

"Give her a few days. She'll cool off," Horace said.

"Let's play some more cards and drink more wine," I said, trying not to feel sorry for myself.

I wanted to call Mary, but I didn't have her phone number.

After playing cards for a while and listening to Horace tell dirty jokes, I started feeling better. I was pretty drunk by the time I was ready to go to sleep, and I almost passed out immediately. Horace and Melanie decided to spend the night. They didn't feel like walking home.

In the morning, I was resolved to apologize to Mary. John and I walked to school together. As we passed the statue of David, it looked distraught to me, as if David's battle was more internal, rather than a battle with an external force. John and Pat were getting along fine; he had waited and chosen the woman he liked the most and was making it work. I was trying to learn from him, but I couldn't decide on one woman, except Monica, who was aloof.

Horace and Melanie had left our apartment earlier and were sitting in the café when we arrived. Mary was sitting with them.

"Hi," I said, looking at Mary.

"Hi," she said, in a pleasant tone.

I wondered if Horace had said something to her. I was willing to bet he had. I sat down after ordering my usual double cappuccino and patted Mary's hand briefly.

"I'm sorry about last night," I said.

"It's okay. We had a little too much to drink," she said.

Horace was smiling; he had smoothed everything over, and I was grateful. After thinking about it, I was glad that Mary had resisted my advances, because I knew I would have just taken her for granted. We chatted for a while, and everything was fine, until Monica walked in. Horace nodded to me, and I turned around to notice Monica with an Italian guy we had never seen before.

"Hi, Monica," Horace said with a smirk on his face.

"Hi, guys," she said, and immediately turned to her friend.

Rumors abounded in our little school, and some of the gossip was vicious. I heard from John and Jesse that I was already getting a reputation as a womanizer, which didn't bother me much, except that it fueled Monica's resistance toward me. Now it seemed she had a boyfriend, but why she had brought him to school I couldn't figure out, until later, when I discovered that he was modeling for her. I was giving up on Monica, but not completely. For now I would concentrate on Mary.

Mary and I began chatting about the weather and our beautiful city, but soon we got into a serious discussion.

"I don't tell many people this, but I had a nervous breakdown when I was nineteen," I said, while looking down at my feet.

"What prompted it?" she said.

"I was stressed out at school, and I had trouble sleeping. Instead of getting exhausted, like everybody else, and eventually falling asleep, I got manic and my thoughts were racing all the time, making it impossible for me to sleep," I said.

"Then what happened?" she said.

"Well, after a few days not sleeping, I began to have psychotic thoughts, and my brother and father took me to the hospital," I said.

She was silent for a minute, and I could tell by the expression on her face that she was sympathetic to my story.

"I'm fine now. I've been well for a long time," I said.

"You seem perfectly normal. Are you on medication?" she said.

"I was for a while, but I stopped taking it against my doctor's advice. I sleep fine now. I'm not worried about it happening again," I said.

"I'm glad you recovered fully," she said. "Don't breakdowns affect people for the rest of their lives sometimes?"

"Most people never recover fully. I'm lucky. Now I have to take measures to keep it from happening again," I said.

"Did you suffer a great deal?" she asked.

"Ironically enough, when you are manic, you feel really good, and coming down on the medication isn't too bad. I was manic for a couple of months after I was released from the hospital, and came down slowly. All things considered, I really didn't suffer at all."

Her face turned to relief, and a smile crept over her.

"Now you have something to write about," she said.

"That's true, but I'm going to wait a while to put it into perspective," I said.

Mary and I talked some more and ended up skipping all our classes. We went to lunch and enjoyed the outdoor atmosphere of a downtown restaurant. I watched the passersby and absorbed the ambience of the bustling city. Italians are always in a hurry, probably because they drink so much coffee. The sun filtered through distant light clouds, brightening the streets and reflecting off slanted windows across the piazza.

"I want to say something about last night," Mary said.

"Please don't. I understand perfectly. I was moving much too fast," I said.

"I just got upset, because I know you've already slept with a couple of women in our program, and I don't want to be just another notch on your belt," she said.

"I really like you, Mary. I wouldn't have told you so many personal things today if I didn't like you. Something you should know about men is that we're all horny, and the way we become intimate with women is to sleep with them," I said.

"Not all men become intimate with women by sleeping with them. That's ridiculous," she said.

"Maybe I should just speak for myself," I said.

"Well, you shared a lot of intimate things with me today, but you haven't slept with me," she said.

"That's true, but it's unusual for me," I said.

After lunch we parted ways, and I went to a little thirteenth century church to look at the early influences of Renaissance architecture. I had decided not to ask Mary over for dinner. I thought it would be better to slow down. No one was around in the church, so I sat in the back and looked at the various features of architecture. An hour later, I walked through the open market downtown and bought some fresh food for dinner. Jesse was home when I arrived; we decided to play a few hands of pitch. He talked about his new girlfriend, and I talked about Mary. Jesse was very shy. He wouldn't dare kiss his new friend or try to touch her, and I told him his shyness would work for him as long as he talked to her and kept showing interest.

"I'm falling in love with her, Paul. I can't control my emotions," he said.

"Take your time. You lack experience. You're going to have your heart broken if you don't protect yourself," I said.

"I want to marry her," he said.

"Whoa, boy. Take it easy. You just met her. Get to know her first. There are a lot of things about an individual that you have to know before you make a commitment. Besides, you're too young to be so serious," I said.

He stared out the window, probably thinking about her and imagining the future. I chuckled to myself, because I was the same way. As soon as I was infatuated, I was already planning out the next twenty years.

"What about Mary?" he said.

"What about her?" I said.

"How do you feel about her?" he said.

"I like her, but I'm not in love," I said.

"You have a lot more experience than I do," he said. "You keep a cooler head and don't fall in love as easily."

"I think I'm in love with Monica, but she doesn't want anything to do with me," I said.

"How can you be in love with someone that you're not going out with?" he said.

"You are naïve," I said nicely. "I'm usually in love with someone other than whom I'm dating."

He thought about that for a minute and seemed to understand it intellectually, but not deep down. We started making dinner; we didn't know if Horace and Melanie were going to show up, but we were hungry, so we began cooking. We always experimented with new pasta dishes. I had bought some shrimp and scallops, so we sautéed those in butter first and cooked the noodles separately. We decided to make a white sauce, melting the cheese and butter and slowly adding the heavy cream. By the time we were finished, everybody started showing up. Horace and Melanie didn't even ring the doorbell. They just walked in. Horace had a big smile on his face.

"Well, I guess I don't have to cook tonight," he said.

I noticed he had brought two bottles of wine, and dinner was almost ready, so we opened the wine and started drinking. By the time we finished eating, I had consumed four glasses of wine and was feeling pretty good. Melanie felt tired and went home early. Horace and I wanted to walk around town and decided to bring a bottle of wine with us. We walked to a little international bar where students from all over the world gathered to play chess and drink.

We had finished the bottle of wine by the time we arrived, and we were laughing almost hysterically, so we walked in the quiet bar. Horace was naturally loud, but after a few drinks, his voice went up a notch. We quieted down a little and sat with a couple of blonde women who were talking animatedly with each other. Unlike the States, where there is always room for everybody, in Italy you share tables, which afforded us the opportunity to sit with these extremely attractive women.

We ordered a couple of glasses of wine and continued our conversation, noticing that the women were speaking in German. After a few minutes, Horace and I introduced ourselves, and were relieved to discover that they both spoke English. The woman sitting next to Horace was named Greta. She was tall with long, golden hair cascading over her shoulders. The other was named Anna, and she was a little shorter, with curly blonde hair and a dazzling smile.

The four of us talked about how beautiful Florence was, and how warm it was compared to Germany. The women seemed interested in us, and we soon paired off, Horace with Greta, and I with Anna. Anna was an architecture student, and I soon found out that the women shared an apartment not too far away.

"They live right around the corner," I said to Horace.

"Let's take the party to your place," Horace suggested to them.

They agreed, and we were soon escorting them through the narrow streets of the city to their place. They lived in a tiny little apartment on the first floor, not too far from the river. The two women shared a bedroom, and the apartment was furnished with very old pieces, though they were not antiques.

"How did you find this place?" I asked Anna.

"It was in the newspaper. A friend of ours saw it," she said.

Greta brought out a bottle of wine and put on some jazz, as we got cozy in their small living room. Horace entertained us with some wild stories from the Deep South, and after a while, we were pretty drunk. Anna asked me if I wanted to see her art portfolio and gently dragged me into the bedroom. Before I got a chance to see any drawings, we were on the bed, making out passionately. The German women had a reputation for being pretty wild, but I was still surprised to find myself in that position after knowing Anna for only an hour or two.

"How long has it been since you've made love?" I said.

"Six months!" she exclaimed, as she took off my shirt.

Ironically enough, I felt like she was taking advantage of me, and I realized immediately what Mary must have felt like. I was pretty drunk though and just went along for the ride, not worried about how I would feel later.

"You have a nice body," she said.

"You do too," I said, as I voraciously began sucking on her tits.

She pushed me over and sucked my cock. It had been so long for her that she attacked me, pulling my ass toward her, thrusting my cock deep in the back of her throat. We were like animals, not thinking about anything, just devouring each other's bodies with a hunger that had to be satisfied.

"I want to fuck you in the ass," I said, thinking about the fun I had had with Laura.

"I don't do that," she said.

"How about if you stick your finger up my ass?" I slurred.

"What's with the ass?" she laughed.

"Forget it," I said, diving down to her cunt and licking her with gusto.

"I want you inside me," she said.

"I want to fuck you from behind," I said.

"Just put it in the right hole," she teased.

I rolled her over and slapped her ass gently, asking her to help me slip inside. She had a beautiful plump ass, and I pounded it with fury, feeling almost anger in my thrusts. She groaned deeply, gasping for breath. We weren't using any contraceptives, so I pulled out just before I came. I knew I was still taking a risk, but at that point I didn't care. Exhausted, I rolled over and stared at the ceiling, catching my breath, while she masturbated to orgasm. I could hear Horace going at it in the other room and thought I would stay put for a few minutes.

"How do you feel?" I said.

"Wonderful," she said. "You're quite the animal," she scolded.

I felt totally unsatisfied, as though I had just been taken advantage of. She rolled over and went to sleep, and I crept into the living room to find Horace getting dressed. He had a self-satisfied look on his face. I wondered how he could feel good about cheating on Melanie, but I didn't say anything. I didn't feel good, probably because I felt I was cheating on Mary.

Horace and I split up outside, walking home in different directions. I was bushed and not feeling well, and I was very pleased to collapse on my bed.

Chapter Twelve

The next morning I dragged myself out of bed, washed my hair, and walked down to the local café for a double espresso. Instead of taking the bus, I walked to school, thinking the walk would make me feel better. I swore to myself that I would never get drunk again.

By the time I arrived at school, I had already missed my first class, so I sat down in the café with Horace and rehashed the night before. It amazed me how he could drink so much and feel perfectly fine the next day.

"How was she?" Horace said.

"All right I guess. She attacked me, and I just went along for the ride," I said.

Horace laughed and told me his experience had been delightful. He recounted some details of his experience, and I laughed when he told me he came all over her face. Obviously, he felt no guilt. Apparently, he felt he loved Melanie, and these sexual exploits were more entertainment. I'm sure Melanie didn't feel the same way, but we never talked about it. I wondered if I would be that way after getting married, but I didn't think so.

"Are you going to see Anna again?" he asked me.

"I don't know. I doubt it," I said.

A few minutes later, Mary got out of class and walked into the café. She gave me a great big smile, and I smiled too, though I felt uneasy. She ordered a cappuccino and sat down with us.

"You look tired," she said.

"I was up late," I answered.

She looked at Horace, who winked at her, and Mary said:

"So you guys went out last night and probably got into some trouble."

"A little," I said.

She smiled knowingly, but I figured she would never guess what we had been up to. We only chatted for a few minutes, until it was time to go to the next class. I asked Mary if she wanted to have dinner with us a couple of nights later, and she agreed. I was counting on Horace to keep his mouth shut, but you never knew with him. I wasn't in love with Mary, but I was getting attached to her, like a sister.

That afternoon, I hung around the school, hoping to get a chance to talk to Monica, who spent the afternoons in her studio. She had a "do not disturb" sign on her door, so I hung around the café, waiting for her to take a break. Finally, she came down for a cup of coffee, after I had sat there for an hour, and she gave me a surprised look, knowing that I didn't usually hang around school so late. I was reading one of my Italian novels when she walked in.

"What's up, Paul? Nothing going on this afternoon?"

"I need to catch up on my reading. I haven't done any homework in a while. The guys are too distracting at home," I said.

"What are you reading?" she said.

"*The Baron in the Trees*," I said.

"Is it good?" she said.

"It's great. It's about a young man who one day climbs a

tree in a forest and never comes down again. He lives in the trees and has a girlfriend who lives on the ground," I said.

"That's different," she said.

"It was intended to give a completely different perspective on life, like the other modern novels of the time," I said.

Monica had paint on her smock, and I knew she wasn't going to take a long break, so I asked her if she wanted to come over for dinner sometime soon. She agreed, but we didn't set a date.

I left school feeling that I was wasting my time with Monica, but she had dug under my skin, and I didn't want to let her go. The city was bustling as usual, and I started to feel more elated as I walked through the beautiful, narrow streets. I stopped in a small shop and bought my favorite soft cheese, which you could spread on bread, and eat for a snack. Then I stopped to buy some wine and searched all over for a special vintage that I finally found.

When I arrived at the apartment, John and Jesse were playing cards. They were glad to see me with the wine. We played our usual hands of pitch and drank a little wine with the cheese. The three of us were getting very close, as we spent most of our free time together. While we played cards, we always discussed our love lives. Jesse and John were entertained by my fickle ways. Jesse was getting serious with his German girlfriend, and I thought they might even get married one day. John and Pat were going pretty steady, but he was a cool customer. I knew he wasn't thinking about marriage.

"You're late today. What have you been up to?" John said to me.

"I hung around school to get a minute alone with Monica, so that I could ask her over for dinner. I'm not getting anywhere with her. I can tell by her indifference," I said.

"She's a tough one," Jesse said.

"Is she coming over for dinner?" John said.

"Yeah, but we didn't set a date; Mary is coming over the day after tomorrow," I said.

"You crack me up," John said.

"I amuse myself too," I said.

"Well, at least you can laugh at yourself," Jesse said.

We never played cards for money, because we weren't gamblers, and we had just enough money for living expenses, but our games were very competitive. We kept score, and the winner had bragging rights. We became close friends by spending our free time together, and at school we were known as the three musketeers.

At dinnertime, right on schedule, Horace showed up. Melanie had stayed home to study, and Horace was all excited about being a free man. He cooked a special white sauce with chicken, and we started with big plates of pasta. Unlike Henry Miller, I never felt hungry while in Europe, because, of course, my parents were subsidizing my trip. We always ate well and always had a bottle of wine to go with dinner.

Horace wanted to roam the city again at night, but I told him I had studying to do. The truth was, I really wanted to go to bed early and get a fresh start in the morning. It was pouring with rain that night, but Horace insisted on going out. Neither John nor Jesse wanted to go out, so Horace went alone.

The next morning, in the café, I heard all about his wild night. He had gotten drunk, naturally, and had gone back to the opium den. He said he didn't partake of any drugs, but you never knew with him. A woman had approached him, and he had taken her back to a secluded spot for a blowjob. After receiving a hell of a blowjob, as he put it, Horace had put his hand up her dress only to discover that this "woman" had a great big cock. I never laughed so hard in all my life.

"I decided to punch the guy out," Horace said, and he told me how he broke the guy's nose.

"Maybe it would be a good idea if you didn't go back there any more," I said.

"I think you're right," he smiled.

Chapter Thirteen

The next night, Mary came over for dinner, and to my surprise, Monica showed up too. John had invited Monica, forgetting that I had scheduled Mary for that night. It was not a big deal, but I wanted to have Monica come over by herself, so that I could talk to her alone after dinner. Mary and Monica were not close friends, but I noticed Monica making a concerted effort to talk to Mary and include her in the conversation. Horace knew the situation only too well, but he was unusually discreet in everything that he said. We played some cards after dinner, and the evening turned out to be very pleasant. Horace, Melanie, and Monica left at about nine, but Mary stayed behind.

Mary and I went into my bedroom to be alone, and I could tell there was something on her mind.

"Monica is so sweet," Mary said.

"She's really nice," I said.

"I know how you feel about her," she said.

"What do you mean?" I said.

"I know you're infatuated with her, and that you want to go out with her," she said.

I stammered for a second and then foolishly denied it.

"Paul, don't lie. I know you like her. It's okay, really. I don't mind," she said.

"Who did you hear that from?"

"Word gets around."

"Well, if it makes you feel any better, she's not interested in me."

"I don't know about that," Mary said.

"I do," I said.

I turned on the radio, and we listened to some popular Italian music. I missed my stereo and my American music. Later, I would buy a small tape player and listen to music from the States.

Mary was in an amorous mood, and we started kissing. I didn't want to be too aggressive, and I let her take my shirt off. It wasn't long before we were completely naked and began oral sex. She was good at sucking cock. She liked to tease me with her tongue for a while before enveloping me completely. Her pussy was so clean and tender; it tasted so good. We ate each other out slowly, savoring every delicious nibble and lick. It was not the passionate lovemaking of lovers; it was more like the exploration of youthful bodies. Unlike D.H. Lawrence's lovers, we were not shaking the earth but just having fun in our youthful way. I was watching her suck my cock, and I imagined Monica doing it. I could see her fine blonde hair flowing over my thighs. Mary was somewhat inexperienced, but she had imagination and a desire to learn. I asked her to lick my anus, and she was willing to do it, giving me the greatest pleasure.

After a long time of oral sex, I rolled her over on her stomach and fucked her from behind. She had a plump little ass, and it felt great rubbing up against it. I stopped as I approached orgasm and waited until I calmed down. Then I started again slowly, saving myself. Finally, I couldn't wait any longer, and I slammed her until I came. She screamed out a little, and then we lay their silently catching our breath. We fell asleep a short time later and slept in each other's arms the rest of the night.

Chapter Fourteen

Several weeks later, I was talking to our librarian, who was a gorgeous Italian woman, and she invited me on a retreat with some of her friends. She was about my age. Her name was Gabriela, and she was tall and slender with long, dark, curly hair. I could tell she was flirting with me, so I asked her if she had a boyfriend. She said no, which got my dirty mind thinking. We were to go out into the countryside to a villa about thirty minutes outside of Florence.

On Saturday, I packed a lunch early and waited for Gabriela to pick me up. When I told John about going on the retreat, I thought he would be critical, but he was all in favor of it, realizing that we didn't socialize with the Italians enough.

Gabriela was downstairs, beeping the horn at eight o'clock sharp. We had spent some time talking the last few days, and I realized she really had a crush on me. Driving through the countryside was a true joy. I hadn't been in a car in a long time, and I almost asked her if I could drive. The hills outside of Florence are truly magnificent, and the roads wind their way around and around, affording spectacular views.

She was very talkative, describing all her friends to me and their various pursuits. She was wearing a short skirt, because it was an unusually warm October day, and I kept staring at her sexy long legs. We spoke in Italian, because her English was very broken.

"Are you in school now, Gabriela?" I asked.

"Yes, I'm at the University studying architecture."

"I see a lot of the buildings going up are traditionally built. Is there a great need for architects?" I said.

"Not really," she said. "I'm just trying to get a degree so that I can get some type of regular job."

"You look very athletic. Do you play any sports?" I said.

"I play tennis," she said.

"So do I. We should play sometime."

"Sure, there are some courts not far from Piazza Savonarola," she said.

Even though our cultures were different, I felt we had a lot to talk about. She was very lively and quick to reveal her dazzling smile. I was turning my head a great deal, I noticed, alternating from the beautiful view outside, and the one inside. I was not really nervous around her, but I was trying to make a good impression.

"Do you like Italian literature?" I said.

"Very much so, but I also love English literature and some of the contemporary novels from Eastern Europe and South America."

"You should visit me sometime in the States," I said.

"Oh, I would love to. Do you mean it?"

"Absolutely," I said.

We weren't planning on spending the night out in the country, but I wondered if we would be able to have some time alone together. Finally, we arrived at this beautiful villa, perched on the side of a hill, surrounded by finely manicured gardens. The view from the house was spectacular. A few cars were there already, and we spent the first few minutes meeting everybody. She was good about not abandoning me, and she stuck by my side most of the time.

Her friends were great. I discovered that most of them were attending the University, mostly because there weren't any jobs. At one point, after lunch, Gabriela and I went for a long walk around the hills. We sat under a tree and got to know each other better. I really liked her, and all I could think about was kissing her.

"Do you want to live in Italy?" she asked.

"Not for the rest of my life, but I would like to spend a year here now and again," I said.

She seemed disappointed; maybe she had visions of us living together. I knew it would be difficult to go out with her for only a short while, without at least attempting to make a long-term commitment. I looked out at the great vista, and I wondered where I would be in twenty years. Commitment was impossible at that time; there was so much to do, so many places to go. I couldn't image settling down.

"I would like to live in America," she said, "at least for a little while."

"Well, if you come to visit, I'll help you find a job teaching Italian, and we'll find you an apartment," I said.

"I would like to see New York," she said.

"New York is fascinating; it's the most interesting city in the world," I said.

Her eyes had a dreamy look. She was imagining our great country, which I just took for granted. I was in love with Italy, but I didn't know that some day I would be torn between the two countries. Suddenly, I had the urge to kiss her and only hesitated for a moment. She responded with a passionate embrace, and our tongues were playing gently with each other. I was afraid to go further and was satisfied with half an hour of intense kissing.

"You have a girlfriend, don't you?" she said.

"Sort of," I said, "but we're not in love," I added.

"Men lie all the time." She laughed.

I tried kissing her again, but she said that was enough. We walked back to the villa and played some games with the others. There was very little drinking, and several of the guests prepared a lavish dinner.

In the evening, exhausted, we drove back to Florence. I kissed her goodnight but didn't make a date for the future. I liked her quite a bit, and as soon as she dropped me off, I began comparing her to Mary. I liked the way Gabriela kissed better than Mary, but Mary seemed more independent. Then there was Monica. I couldn't compare women at that time without thinking about Monica. John was still up when I got home, and he wanted all the details of the excursion. He laughed when I told him I had made out with Gabriela.

"Is she a good kisser?" he asked.

"Great," I said, "but I was afraid to go any further."

"She's probably not as fast as the American women," he said.

"That's what I thought," I said.

"You love to complicate things, don't you?" he said.

"I might as well play the field while I'm young," I said.

"Mary's going to find out," he said.

"It was innocent enough," I said.

"She may not feel that way," he said.

Chapter Fifteen

The following morning, refreshed from a deep sleep, I went jogging before school. I had to dodge cars, even that early in the morning, but I was full of energy and ready to seize the day.

When I got to school, Horace was sitting in his usual spot, already telling stories. He smiled at me as I sat down, but continued to finish his story. Jesse and John were sitting with him, and Ellen was at the next table listening in. Several other students were milling about, but Monica and Mary were nowhere to be seen.

"You're in trouble," Horace said to me after he finished his story.

"Why?" I asked.

"Mary found out you spent yesterday with our librarian." He laughed.

"Oh geeze," I said.

Just then, Monica and Mary walked in together and stood at the coffee bar, totally ignoring me. Horace looked at me and laughed again.

"You'd better say something," he said.

"I don't know what to say."

I walked up to the bar and said:

"Hi, ladies."

Neither of them said a word to me. I shook my head and left for class. I could hear Horace laughing as I walked out. Instead of participating in class, I wrote a letter to Mary. I apologized and insisted my day with Gabriela had been perfectly innocent. I was planning on giving her the letter after class, but I decided to rip it up instead. I would apologize to her in person. I was beginning to get a bad reputation around school as a womanizer, and word traveled quickly around our small school. Even more than Mary's silence, Monica's attitude toward me bothered me. After class I decided to talk to Ellen. I was hoping she could help me out.

"Hi, Paul," she said, as I sat down next to her in the café.

"At least you're talking to me," I said.

"Why not?" she said.

"Mary's mad at me and won't talk to me."

"What did you do?" she said.

"Nothing. I just went on a retreat with Gabriela, but it was perfectly innocent."

Ellen had a smile on her face and watched Mary on the other side of the room talking to Monica.

"Want me to say something to her?" she said.

"You read my mind, Ellen. Would you tell her it was perfectly innocent and that I'm sorry if I hurt her feelings?"

"Sure."

Ellen walked over to Mary and talked to her for a minute. At one point, Mary turned around and flipped her middle finger at me. I walked over to them and said:

"Mary, I'm sorry. I don't even know what I did wrong."

"Don't even talk to me," she said.

I left the café in a huff, and I heard Monica giggle. Horace was outside having a cigarette. He saw the expression on my face.

"What's the matter, Paul?" he said.

"Mary's being a bitch," I said.

"Maybe you deserve it."

"I probably do," I said, with a slight smile.

"Come one," he said. "Let's get out of here."

"With pleasure," I said.

We started walking with no particular destination in mind. Whenever I had problems with women, I relied on my male friends for support. It was a brisk day, and the sun was shining, brightening my mood considerably. Horace kept a fast pace, as if he had an appointment or something.

"We've got a week off coming up," I said. "We need to plan a trip."

"Where should we go," he said.

"I'd like to go south where the weather is good," I said.

"Who should we go with?" he said.

"I'd like to go with you and Melanie and maybe Mary, if she's talking to me by then," I said.

"Four of us would be good," he said. "Any more and it would be problematic."

I watched a beautiful Italian woman sitting on her motorbike, talking to a friend of hers, and I thought that maybe I would say something to her.

"Leave her alone," Horace said.

"You wouldn't, if you could speak the language." I laughed.

"That's true," he smiled.

We went to the open market downtown, where the hustle and bustle of the city was focused. It was a great pleasure just walking around, looking at the leather jackets and other wares, and of course looking at the beautiful women. Horace wanted to buy a pair of wool pants, as the weather was getting colder, and his wardrobe wasn't Italian enough. As he looked for pants, I struck up a conversation with an American woman who was attending another program in the city. She was having trouble with the restrictions her family was putting on her, so I suggested that she rent her own apartment with friends, like we were doing.

Horace came to the apartment with me just to hang out and play cards. I decided to call Mary and have it out with her.

"Hello?" she answered.

"This is Paul," I said.

"What's up?" she said in a cold voice.

"I just want to explain," I said.

"No need to. I understand perfectly."

"What do you understand?" I said.

"That you're an asshole."

"Why?" I said.

"I don't want to talk about it," she said, and hung up the phone.

I put down the receiver and shook my head.

"She's not having it, huh?" Horace said.

"I'm in real trouble," I said.

"Good for her," he said.

"Whose side are you on, Horace?"

"Hers." He laughed.

"You should talk, the way you behave," I said.

"Melanie gives me hell too. That's the way it goes," he said.

"Our vacation is in two weeks, and I really want Mary to go with us," I said.

"She'll cool off by then," Horace said.

We played cards for a while, until Jesse and John showed up. We decided to go down to the café on the corner and play pinball. I couldn't stop thinking about what Mary had said to me; my feelings were really hurt. I figured Monica hated my guts too, which made me feel worse. I had to get back with Mary somehow, and I wasn't willing to simply wait until she cooled off.

Chapter Sixteen

I left the guys at the café and walked all the way to Mary's house, which was at least two miles away. When she answered the door, she gave me a nasty look.

"Come on. How long are you going to stay mad?" I said.

"For the rest of your life," she said.

She let me in the door, and before I could make my speech, she started kissing me. I was so surprised that I just stood there without responding.

"I thought you were still mad," I said.

"Anybody who walks all the way here deserves a kiss," she laughed.

"Nothing happened between me and Gabriela," I said.

"That's because she wouldn't let you," she said. "I don't want to talk about it any more. You don't appreciate me enough," she added.

Her family wasn't at the apartment, so we decided to make up. She dragged me into her tiny bedroom, onto the small bed, and started ripping my clothes off. I told her to leave her panties on. She was so sexy that way. She began sucking my cock right away and made loud, slurping sounds, which made me laugh. She was so into it, I asked her to lick my anus, and she did with gusto. I was so hard that it hurt when she pushed down on my cock. I was about to come as she licked my ass and stroked my cock, so I stopped her and flung her down on her stomach. I entered her from behind and pumped wildly until I came. She hadn't had an orgasm, but she said she didn't care. She was glad I got off.

We talked for a long time afterwards, and I told her I wanted her to go with us to Southern Italy. She got all excited about the trip; we took out a map of Italy and started planning. I wanted to go to Capri, where I had been before, and she wanted to go to Sicily, where so many interesting Greek and Roman ruins were located. She came to dinner that night. Horace was pleased we were back together. At dinner, Mary and Melanie took out the map and discussed all the different places we might go. I had found out we could get a student rate to take the train, for a very reasonable price. Melanie wanted to see Pompeii, which was easy to include in our itinerary, since we were going to Capri, right off the shore of Naples.

We drank wine late into the night and planned our trip. We decided to skip half a week of school and extend our trip to ten days. I was responsible for getting the train tickets, and Melanie made reservations for hotels, though there were many places we didn't even make reservations. John and Jesse had decided to go to Paris for their vacation, and Patricia was going to Germany with a friend of hers.

Two weeks later, the four of us departed for Naples on a very crowded train. We stopped in Rome, where most of the passengers got off, and the rest of the ride was more comfortable, because we could actually sit down. Horace and I drank a little wine on the trip; we didn't get drunk, but we laughed all the way to Naples, as he told his great stories of the Deep South.

We were told to watch our wallets around Naples, as it was full of thieves. The warm sun was out when we arrived in the late afternoon, and we immediately climbed into a cab to go to the hotel. I noticed the difference between Naples and the northern cities immediately. Naples seemed much older and not kept up very well, as it was poorer. It still had a great deal of charm, but it was not nearly as elegant as Rome and Florence.

Melanie had made reservations in a small hotel, and it turned out to be pretty run down, though the price was unbeatable. When Horace saw their room, he rolled his eyes and said:

"Why don't we just spend one night here and stay in Capri tomorrow night."

"Good idea," Mary said.

The beds were very soft, and sank down in the middle. They were twin beds instead of double beds, so Mary and I pushed the beds together, thinking it would be like a double bed, but we were wrong. We didn't sleep very well that night, because we were excited abut the trip and not used to being on the road. We made love three times, and by the morning were completely spent. She wanted to suck my cock again when we woke up, but I begged for mercy, since it was too sore.

Horace got up early and was already at the café on the corner of our block. I dragged myself into the shower, and later went to the café with Mary to join the other two.

"Man, you look like you've been through hell," Horace said.

"Those beds were terrible. We didn't get any sleep," I said.

"That's not the reason though," Horace quipped.

We packed up our bags after breakfast and rode a bus to the pier, where the boats departed for Capri. A man tried to sell us a watch on the pier as we waited for our boat, but we didn't fall for it. The boat ride was very uncomfortable, and Melanie threw up over the side but felt better afterwards. I hadn't been on a boat for a long time, and our short trip on the water was exciting. The sky was clear. We could see the two or three islands off the coast, as well as Mount Vesuvius.

I had been to Capri with my mother years earlier, so I knew the best place to stay was on top of the island in a little village called Onscapri.

"We need to buy some wine here," Horace said. "There's a hint of sulfur in it, which makes it very interesting."

"How do you know this stuff?" I said.

He just winked and smiled. There were small buses that went to Onscapri, and the ride up the mountain was as frightening as any roller coaster. The view from the bus was spectacular. The hills cascading toward the sea were dotted with picturesque white houses and rows of olives and grapes. Melanie took pictures from the bus, but trees along the narrow road obscured many views.

I was tired out but excited at the same time. When we arrived at the village, we walked up to a woman to ask her where a good, cheap hotel was, and she turned out to be English. She was so happy to speak to us; she gave us her phone number and invited us over for dinner. She gave us directions to a beautiful pensione, and we were thrilled with the accommodations. The beds were much firmer; Mary and I collapsed in them immediately.

After a very long nap, Mary and I took a shower together and walked out on our balcony to observe the view. From our second story room, we could see many backyards with fruit trees and flowers, but we couldn't see the ocean. We went next door, but Horace and Melanie had gone out. We strolled to the village and walked along the shops to look at the interesting wares. The afternoon was spent just getting used to our surroundings.

When we got back to the hotel, Horace was sitting in the garden outside, sipping a glass of wine, reading a book.

"How do you like this place?" I said.

"Marvelous," Horace said, "and this wine is really delicious."

Mary went to find Melanie, and I joined Horace for a glass of wine. The four of us got dressed up and walked down the steep hill to join the English woman and her husband for dinner. She rarely had a change to speak English, so she talked most of the evening about European history. It was a very educational and enjoyable evening.

Mary and I were tired when we got back to the hotel, and I immediately went to sleep. We didn't awaken until eight thirty the next day, and I attacked her before she had a chance even to brush her teeth. We made love frantically and more passionately than usual, kissing with tenderness and force at the same time. She made more noise than usual too, groaning deeply when she reached orgasm. At one point, she pinched my cock below the head, preventing me from coming, and then gently guided me back inside. Finally, I came, and we collapsed.

"Well, we got our exercise for the day," I said.

"I love your energy," she said.

"Come on. Let's take a shower and go downstairs to meet Horace," I said.

Horace was sipping his cappuccino out in the garden, and Melanie was reading the local paper.

"This is the life," Horace said.

"What are we doing today?" I said.

"We're going to try to see the blue grotto," Melanie said. "It depends on how wavy it is."

We sat enjoying our coffee. The birds walked around from table to table looking for crumbs. A beautiful canary was singing in a fruit tree, and I felt that this was the way the whole world should be. Mary had a wonderful glow in her face. She looked contented and at peace. The sky was a deep blue, dotted with puffy white clouds, and the air smelled of the salty ocean.

We took a taxi down to the blue grotto, but it was too wavy, so it was closed. There was a church I wanted to see, with a tiled floor depicting the Garden of Eden. We went to see that, and it was spectacular. After that, we walked around the town for a while and decided we would leave the island the next day. We were disappointed we didn't get a chance to see the blue grotto, but we saw most everything else on the island.

"I want to see Pompeii," Mary said to me that evening. "I've been studying the artwork and relics for so long; it would be fascinating to walk around them."

"We're going tomorrow for sure, if it's open," I said.

Horace and I stayed up late that evening in the garden, drinking a couple of bottles of wine. The women went to bed early. I had never seen Horace so mellow, and it was easier to talk to him that night because he wasn't trying to entertain me.

"Things look good between you and Mary," he said. "Are you falling in love with her?"

"I don't think so, but I am enjoying her company. It feels like we're a married couple on this trip, but I don't know how I'm going to feel when we get back to Florence," I said.

"You're still obsessed with Monica, aren't you?" he said.

"I guess so, but I haven't thought about her much lately," I said.

He poured me another glass of wine, because he wanted me to keep up with him. I could feel the effects of the wine, but I wasn't really drunk, or at least I didn't feel it until I got up to go to the bathroom. The stars were out, and the neighborhood was perfectly quiet.

"Melanie and I aren't really getting along," he said.

"I haven't noticed it," I said.

"We don't show it, but she's very upset with me," he said.

"Why?" I said.

"The cheating thing," he said.

I just nodded and thought that I was basically having the same problem.

"Maybe it's time to quit drinking," I said, as I took a drink.

"I'm not ready for that," he said.

I looked up at the sky to see a crescent moon, and took a deep breath of fresh air. I wondered what it would be like to live in Capri, somewhat disconnected from the world, watching time pass slowly. I imagined that living there in the summers would be better, and having an apartment in Florence or Rome.

"What are you going to do when you get back to the States?" I asked, knowing they were leaving Italy in a month.

"I'll get a job as a chef somewhere, and Melanie will finish school," he said.

"Maybe I'll come down south to write a novel," I said, which actually happened a year later.

"Yeah, you should come down; there are lots of jobs, and the area around Raleigh is full of schools," he said.

"How are the women?" I said.

"Best women in the world," he said.

"Perhaps I could get a job waiting on tables where you're cooking," I said.

"There are some fine restaurants in Raleigh. You could make quite a bit of money," he said. "Have you been down south at all?"

"I've been to Florida a few times but just on vacation, not for any length of time," I said.

It was getting cooler as we chatted about various things. I went inside and got a sweater. Mary was sound asleep when I entered the room; I stumbled over a chair but didn't wake her up. I hadn't seen Horace in such a serious mood; obviously he was bothered by Melanie. We sat for another hour, telling stories from our past and sharing dreams of the future. Horace wanted to run his own restaurant one day, a fancy place where important people would come to eat. He wasn't good at saving money, so I didn't know how he was going to pull it off.

"Maybe it's time for you to go back to school," I said cautiously.

"I really should," he said.

"There are many programs for hotel and restaurant management," I said.

"No, if I go back, I'll study something else," he said. "I already know everything there is to know about restaurants."

"You'd be a good writer, the way you tell stories," I said.

"I got straight A's in high school," he said.

"You're plenty smart enough," I said, "but it takes discipline and dedication.

I was getting tired, and I was definitely feeling the wine, so I excused myself and went to bed. I slipped into bed without waking Mary and fell sound asleep. The next day we all got up early, and I had a wicked hangover. I took some aspirin, which didn't help, and we packed our bags to resume our trip.

Chapter Seventeen

We stayed on the move the next few days, spending only one night in each town along the southern shore of Sicily. It was paradise. Taormina was extraordinary, built on a mountain overlooking the sea. From the Roman and Greek theatres we could see Mount Etna, snowcapped and silent like a sleeping giant. Horace and Melanie seemed to be getting along, but I noticed they weren't laughing as much as they normally did. At night, the women would go off on their own, while Horace and I would sit outside and drink wine.

Horace and I were becoming very close. We weren't alike in many ways, but our humor meshed perfectly.

One night, sitting by the water in Siracusa, we watched prostitutes strolling up and down the harbor. After a bottle of wine, Horace and I were deep into a discussion about our pasts. I told him I had experienced a nervous breakdown at school and that I was fortunate to have recovered completely, because most patients don't.

"What's it like to be manic?" he asked.

"It happens in stages. First, you start taking on more work than you normally would, and you believe you have powers that no one else has ever had. Then, you get less and less sleep at night, so you're body is very tired, but your mind is racing. Then, at some point, you cross over into a psychotic state," I said.

"What's psychosis like?" he said.

"There are two ways I can describe it. For me, it was like being in a dream. I was anyone I wanted to be, and had no connection with reality. The other way to describe it is it's like being on an acid trip. I was very happy. At times I thought I was God, and that I was the center of the universe," I said.

"I've been close to that," he said. "I've had times when I was strung out on drugs that I had no contact with reality at all."

"The difference is, that after you sleep it off, you're sober again, and the condition doesn't persist," I said.

"Yes, thank God I got off that roller coaster of doing drugs," he said.

I watched the lights of the city dancing on the small waves in front of us. Horace had come from a completely different world than I. He hadn't had the advantages of money and a strong family. He was as intelligent as any person I had ever met, but he was troubled, and he didn't have the calm and composure that is so vital for a happy life. He didn't talk about it, but I'm sure he resented his father, and maybe even his mother, with a deep-seated anger that might have been the cause of his drinking.

"I've got to quit drinking," he said, shaking his head.

"What kind of drugs did you use to do?" I asked.

"You name it; I did it," he said. "I used to deal pot too. Made a lot of money, but I blew it all."

"I love smoking pot," I said.

"Worst drug there is," he said.

"Why?"

"It kills you slowly. Some people stay on it their entire lives and never realize it has killed them," he said.

"I quit it years ago," I said.

"Try not to substitute alcohol for pot, like me," he said.

A prostitute walked up to us and asked us what we were doing. I told her we were married, but "thank you very much." She must have been at least fifty, with deep wrinkles and bags under her eyes. I felt really sorry for her, and after she left, Horace just shook his head. A little later the women joined us for a while. Mary winked at me and said she was going to bed, so I left with her, and we went back to the room all excited to have intense sex.

I was beginning to have strong feelings for Mary, without really being aware of it. That may sound strange, but at that age I had a way of denying my feelings and blocking out emotions that I might not have been able to control. Mary grabbed my ass as we were walking through the door. She took her clothes off immediately. We began with oral sex; she was so excited she thrust my cock deep into the back of her throat. She gagged on it, but thrust it even deeper. I was surprised by her excitement and licked her cunt with just as much passion. After a little while, we calmed down and made love more tenderly. I could feel emotions welling up inside me, tenderness and love that I dismissed as passion. She must have been feeling the same way, because as I was slowly penetrating her, she said:

"I love you so much."

"I love you too," I said, before I had even thought about it.

"You don't," she said.

"I'm starting to feel that way," I said.

"I don't care anyway, I can love you without you loving me," she said.

I was very excited, and I felt like talking dirty, but I didn't. I slammed her with all my might as fast as I could, until I came. It felt so good to squirt my load inside her. I was overwhelmed with pleasure. We were exhausted and went right to sleep without our usual pillow talk.

The next morning, feeling well rested, we took the train to Palermo, our last stop. We weren't too impressed with the city, but there were sections that were very beautiful. We found a nice but inexpensive pensione, and took a nap as soon as we unpacked. When I woke up, I wanted to make love, but Mary wasn't in the mood. Again, we split up; Horace and I walked toward the waterfront, while the women went toward the stores downtown.

"How are you and Melanie getting along?" I asked.

"Better," he said. "We had a long talk last night, and I promised her I would be faithful from now on."

"Can you stick to it?" I said.

"I'm going to try," he said. "I can't afford to lose Melanie. She's the most important person in my life. What about you and Mary?"

"We're really getting along. Our sex life is intense, and it's starting to rub off on our relationship," I said.

"What about Monica?" he said.

"Since we've been away, I haven't thought about her as much, but I know when we get back, I'll be thinking about her all the time," I said.

In the daytime, the waterfront was very busy. Trucks and ships of all kinds crowded the harbor, and the cafés were teeming with people. We sat outside at a small restaurant and talked about everything, particularly women. We ate an early dinner of local fish, and went back to the hotel, though the women still hadn't returned. We played a few hands of cards until the women showed up, loaded with goodies. I went to bed early, while the others stayed up late, drinking wine and laughing.

In the morning, we packed up early and hustled to the train station. We were not looking forward to the fourteen-hour ride back to Florence, but we had our own compartment, so we stretched out and slept most of the time.

Chapter Eighteen

Halfway through the train ride, Mary dragged me into the bathroom and immediately unzipped my pants. She shoved my cock in her mouth and stroked me with her hand at the same time. I came quickly, and she swallowed it greedily.

"Wow! That was the greatest blow job I've ever had," I said.

"Don't forget that when we get home," she said.

We arrived in Florence in the middle of the night, and all hopped into one cab to go to our separate residences. Mary came over to my apartment and slept with me. Early in the morning, we dragged our butts out of bed and got ready for school. It was great to see all our friends again, and the café was loud with stories and laughter. Fortunately, our homework load was very light, because I hadn't looked at a book in two weeks. I talked to Monica for an hour, while Mary was chatting with Melanie, now that they had become close friends.

I realized immediately that I was still obsessed with Monica. She was so much more sophisticated than the other women, and my knees were weak when I talked to her. Mary showed no signs of jealousy, probably because she figured Monica was really not interested.

"Do you want to come over for dinner tomorrow night?" I asked Monica.

"Is Horace cooking?" she said.

"Of course," I said.

"Sure. I'll be there," she said.

I thought I'd better ask Mary to come over as well, or I'd get in trouble. Mary accepted my invitation, and wasn't bothered that I had invited Monica.

The next evening I went to the open market and bought all kinds of fresh food. I wanted it to be a special meal to impress the women. Horace had seen a baked fish dinner at a nice restaurant and wanted to copy it. I bought bluefish and fresh tomatoes and herbs to bake with it, following a list Horace had given me.

Mary came over early, and we opened a bottle of wine. Horace had me preparing some of the food, while Melanie and Mary chatted away. John and Jesse showed up just as we began to cook, and Monica came over a few minutes later. After a few glasses of wine, the talk became very loud, and Horace was the life of the party as usual. Horace made pasta for the first course, with a special red sauce that he had invented.

After a while, I noticed we were all getting pretty drunk. The wine was flowing, and the laughter got louder and louder. After dinner we decided to play cards. We were so drunk we thought we'd play strip poker, though Monica objected at first. We could hardly keep track of the game, although it was obvious Horace was trying to lose on purpose. I lost my shoes after a few minutes, and the women were taking their jewelry off, one piece at a time, which we all thought was cheating. Fortunately, Monica wasn't wearing much jewelry, so after about half an hour, she was down to either her blouse or her skirt. We laughed for ten minutes while she tried to decide what to take off. Finally, she took off her skirt, because she could hide under the table and not be seen.

I rigged the cards a little so that Monica would lose again, but Horace threw away his good cards and lost his pants, leaving him with just his boxers on. Melanie and Mary were hanging on, having worn a lot of jewelry and playing their cards pretty well. I still had my shirt and pants on, and one sock, when Monica lost again. Now it was getting exciting.

"I'm quitting," she said.

"No. You can't," everyone chimed in.

"It's not fair, you guys are cheating," Monica laughed.

"Come on," Horace said, "take it off."

After ten more minutes of arguing, she finally took off her shirt, and we were overjoyed to discover she hadn't worn a bra. We laughed our heads off as she turned redder and redder. She covered herself with her arms, but we all got a good look at her.

"This isn't fair," she kept repeating. "I hardly wore anything!"

Horace lost the next hand and was thrilled to take off his boxers. He strutted around for a few seconds and everyone was in hysterics.

"I lose!" he said several times.

The women were now tired of the game, so we all got dressed and played regular poker for the rest of the evening.

I had fantasies of Monica's breasts all night, and I would have fucked Mary royally, but I had drunk so much I couldn't get it up. I ate her out for a long time though, then rolled over and passed out. In the morning I fondly remembered the dreams I had about Monica, but my head hurt, and reality rushed back in.

Mary and I walked to school together. We were beginning to become a real couple, and I was satisfied to have her as my only girlfriend. We were late; I rushed into my literacy theory class, not quite awake, to hear a very interesting lecture. The professor was talking about the impossibility of repeating a word or anything else, purely.

"Each word, no mater how often repeated, gives off different effects each time, which is why no two writers can ever say the same thing, and why no single writer can ever say the same thing twice, even if he repeats himself word for word," he said.

I thought that was fascinating, and immediately related it to Derrida's version of difference, which I had studied before. I talked to Mary about it after class, but she hadn't found it as interesting as I had. Mary had no intellectual pretensions. She was smart but not interested in complex theories. I went upstairs to Monica's studio and bounced a couple of ideas off her, and she readily agreed with his theory, noting that the effect a painting has on a viewer is actually changing as the viewer studies the painting, and is constantly in motion.

I hadn't realized Monica was so interested in aesthetic theory, and it was just one more reason why I found her to be so appealing. I thought about what Monica had said, and realized that language is in motion, not fixed in time and space, which is why pure repetition is impossible. These thoughts captivated me for the next few hours, as I sat in the café and tried to write some poetry.

I knew Monica was in her studio painting, so I hung around, hoping to run into her. At about three o'clock, she came down from the studio for a cappuccino.

"Are you doing a naked self portrait?" I taunted.

"I'm so embarrassed about last night; everybody is talking about it, and the story is getting very exaggerated!" She laughed.

"It's no big deal. By the way, you look great naked," I said.

She turned red and giggled.

"I would never have done it if I hadn't had so much wine."

"I was surprised you did it," I said, "but pleasantly surprised."

"Did you see Horace? I think he's played before," she said.

"He doesn't need to play cards. He would take his clothes off for no reason at all," I said.

She laughed, and I was captivated by her laughter. She was so relaxed, laughter came easily to her, and her laugh was a beautiful pitch, as beautiful as a bird's song. I was definitely in love. There was no doubt about it, and it was painful to know that it wasn't requited. My mood was perfect for a tragic love poem, and I thought about it even as we talked.

"What are you painting now," I asked.

"I'm doing a colorful abstract piece that moves the eye all over the canvas," she said.

"Is it more difficult to do an abstract painting or a representational one?" I said.

"It depends on the person and their personality; for me, it's easier to do an abstract," she said.

I couldn't even pay attention to what she was saying. I kept watching her deep blue eyes, and the way she tossed her golden hair. I tried to think of something clever to say but, of course, I couldn't. Monica knew I was in love with her, and enjoyed keeping me on that string, tugging every once in a while like a fisherman checking to see if that fish was still on the line. I kept seeing her small, firm breasts jiggling while she laughed. My lust was out of control. I fantasized about kissing her as I watched her lips move. She loved to touch her hair while she talked, curling her locks around her fingers.

"Do you think I could do an abstract painting?" I said.

"Sure, but the first might not look too good. You have to spend some time experimenting with colors and design, because even an abstract painting has to be designed," she said.

"Can I try to paint you?" I said.

"You'd better experiment with somebody else," she laughed. "I don't want to look like a freak!"

I wanted to invite her over for dinner again, without Mary, but after thinking about it for a while, I decided against it. After an hour, I walked home, somewhat disconsolately.

When I got back to the apartment, Horace was drinking and entertaining John and Jesse, and my mood changed immediately. I went to bed fantasizing about Monica and masturbated so that I could fall asleep.

Chapter Nineteen

On some mornings, John and I went jogging. The sun was out that next day, so we went for a little run. I had a great deal of respect for John. He didn't gossip or get involved in anybody else's business. He developed his relationship with Patty and seemed the most content of all of us. I was more carefree, somewhere between John and Horace, at times putting my foot in my mouth, but smoothing it over quickly with something funny. John only laughed loudly after a few drinks. Most of the time he was fairly reserved.

"How are things going with Mary?" John said, as we navigated a narrow street.

"Fine, but I'm still obsessed with Monica."

"Monica is never going to go out with you unless you're single, so you might want to break up with Mary if you're going to make your move," he said.

"You're right. I thought about that, but there's no guarantee Monica would go out with me even if I were single."

I didn't smoke cigarettes at the time, and we were in good shape; our run was pretty long, and extended itself into the countryside.

"Why are you so obsessed with Monica?" he asked.

"I don't know. Why is anybody obsessed with anybody? Probably because she's indifferent toward me."

"If she went out with you for a few months you would probably lose interest," he said.

"I don't know, but I'd like to find out," I said.

We began jogging up the long road toward the fort behind our apartment. It was a slow, gradual climb that took the breath out of us. From those heights, we could see the entire city draped with a light fog. After a while, before reaching the fort, we decided to stop for a few minutes and enjoy the view.

"Are you getting serious about Patricia?" I said.

"We're not getting married or anything, but we'll stick together for the rest of the year," he said.

"See, you did it right. You waited until you decided which one you wanted, and then you got her," I said.

The streets of the city were waking up with loud trucks and cars. We could see the early birds walking toward their favorite cafés. A feeling of deep well-being filled me, and I began joking with John, my sense of humor starting very early that day.

"Why don't you tell Monica that I'm really not interested in her. Maybe the reverse psychology will work," I said.

"I'll tell her that you hate her. Maybe that'll make her fall in love with you," he said.

We jogged back down the hill, realizing we were going to be late for school. I couldn't imagine a more beautiful city, and I thought again that I would live there for the rest of my life. When I got to school, Horace was sitting calmly in the café, waiting for me to arrive.

"Hey, let's play strip poker again. That was fun!" he said.

"You cheat!" I laughed

I got my coffee and went right to class, a few minutes late. I fantasized about Monica and Mary and didn't listen to a word that was said. After class, Mary walked up to me and put her arm around my waist.

"You want to get together tonight?" she said.

"Sure. Why don't you stop over for dinner around eight," I said.

"What panties do you want me to wear?" she whispered in my ear.

"The black ones." I smiled.

I left school early that morning, because I wanted to see a show at a museum that was only there for the day. It was a small museum downtown, and it was an impressionist show of works rarely displayed. A few students from our school were already there when I arrived, including Monica. An early Van Gogh that was dark and gloomy fascinated me, and I asked Monica about his early period. She was an expert in art history and proceeded to give me a long lecture on Van Gogh's development.

I couldn't figure Monica out. She obviously enjoyed spending time with me. We were becoming best friends, but apparently she didn't want to let it go any further. Like Mary, my usual experience was that the women who liked me wanted to be with me. The more she kept me at arm's length, the more I wanted to conquer her.

"Let's go to lunch," I said to her after we left the museum.

"Sure! Are you buying?" she said.

"Of course," I said.

We went to a small trattoria downtown, and ordered pasta. I was determined to confront her in some way about our relationship, but I really didn't know what to say. After a bit of small talk, I said:

"Monica, you seem to like me a great deal. Why won't you go out with me?"

"I am out with you." She smiled.

"You know what I mean! I think we'd make a great couple.

I don't understand you," I said.

"I love you as a friend. Isn't that enough?" she said.

"No, it's not enough," I said.

I stared right at her foolishly, as though I could talk her into something. The restaurant was busy with people, but all I could see or hear was Monica.

"You're not going to persuade me by bullying me," she said.

"I'm sorry, Monica. You just don't know how strongly I feel about you."

"I care about you too, but I've already explained to you why I can't go out with you," she said.

Suddenly, I began to sulk like a child being scolded by his mother.

"I give up," I said.

"Good, now maybe we can make some progress," she said.

"What do mean by that?" I said.

"We need to develop our friendship, and you need to stop lusting after me," she said.

I rolled my eyes. She laughed and reached over to pat my hand. I ate my pasta rapidly and stared at my food. She was casual about eating her dinner, and I believed she enjoyed watching me suffer. I wanted to be cool about it, but I couldn't control my emotions.

"I can't help it if I lust after you!" I said.

"You don't have to drool like a dog. It turns me off," she said.

"I don't drool!" I protested.

She giggled and took a sip of mineral water.

"Besides, I'm starting to date an Italian," she said.

I felt a stab in the heart when she said that. My face turned white, and I surprised myself with my almost violent reaction. I imagined her with a wealthy, very sophisticated and well-dressed man, who was slightly older. Then she told me he was a student at the University of Florence, and I laughed.

"How could a young guy like that possibly interest you?" I said.

"He's very nice and doesn't follow me around," she said defensively.

"Is he handsome?" I asked.

"Pretty handsome," she said. "He's an artist," she added.

I was so jealous. I just shook my head. She had a smug smile on her face, and I immediately wondered if she was telling me a tale.

"You're lying," I said.

"No I'm not," she said.

"Then why don't you bring him around?"

"I will!" she said defiantly.

We ate in silence for the rest of the meal and kissed on the cheek before parting.

I was angry and frustrated as I walked home, and I realized that I was staring at the sidewalk. John was eating when I arrived, and I told him about my lunch with Monica.

"Why don't you give up for a while? That might work," he said.

"I'm going to. That's exactly what I decided on the way home," I said.

Suddenly, I remembered that Mary was coming over that evening. I called Horace, and he agreed to join us. Then I looked in the refrigerator and the cupboards to see if we had enough food. We were out of cheese, and I quickly went to the store around the corner. I knew Horace would bring the wine, and John had invited Patricia, so it looked like another party. Jesse showed up with his girlfriend an hour later with a bottle of wine.

"Jesse, why don't we open that bottle now and have whatever Horace brings later?" I said.

We sat down to play pitch and opened the wine. Jesse had a peculiar smile on his face, and I realized that he probably had just gotten laid. We always drank Chianti, and this was a '77, which was delicious. John took the card game seriously, and Jesse and I were soon far behind. It made me feel better knowing that Mary was probably spending the night, and my sense of humor returned.

A little later, Horace and Melanie arrived with food and wine. Horace immediately opened the bottle and poured everyone another round. He wanted to play strip poker again, but the others declined. Mary came early, and we decided to start cooking. Melanie had brought veal cutlets, which Horace breaded and fried in olive oil.

It didn't take Horace long to drink three or four glasses of wine and begin entertaining everybody. As we sat down to eat, he told one of the most incredible stories I had ever heard.

"When I was still living in the heart of Georgia, I was close friends with a cop who had been on the force only a couple of years. We used to drink together and do a bunch of other drugs, but he was a pretty good guy. One night we were riding around in his patrol car, when we saw two women driving down a deserted road. We though it looked suspicious, so we turned off our headlights and followed them from a distance. They parked off the road by the woods and got out of the car. We snuck up on them and watched them from behind some bushes. They were snorting cocaine, and after a little while, they took their clothes off and started having sex.

"My friend Harry walked over to them quietly and pulled out his gun. When they saw him, they screamed, but he quickly told them to shut up, not that it mattered, because we were in the middle of nowhere," he said.

I watched Melanie as he told this story, wondering what was going through her head, but she just watched him like the others, with a tiny smile on her face.

"Harry took the cocaine and told them he would arrest them if they didn't blow us. We got the most incredible blow jobs, then we fucked them and left with the drugs," he said.

I think Horace was expecting us to laugh, but instead, we stared at him in disbelief.

"I'm just kidding!" he yelled.

Then everybody laughed, but I really wondered if it was a true story or not. We had a great meal, laughing our asses off as Horace did impressions of our professors. Right after dinner, Mary and I excused ourselves and went to my bedroom. We stretched out on the bed, and she immediately unbuttoned my pants and grabbed my cock.

"I've been fantasizing about this all day," she said.

"So have I," I said.

She put her mouth on my cock and slid her hand up and down as she sucked on the head. It was pure ecstasy.

"I love sucking your cock," she said.

"I love it too," I said. "Fuck me in the ass with your finger while you suck me."

"Oh," she said, slowly slipping her finger in my hole.

I loved having a finger up my ass. She moved her hand slowly, sucking hard on my cock. After a minute, I came, even though I didn't want to. In those days, I could wait a few minutes and start all over again.

"I love you," she said, after swallowing my come.

"I love you too," I said, but it was merely an automatic response.

At that age, I could feel a great deal of emotion but, of course, I knew nothing about love.

"Do you like coming in my mouth?" she said.

"It's my favorite thing to do," I said.

I kissed her and slipped two fingers into her pussy, as she stuck her tongue in my ear.

"I love when you flex your ass," she said.

"I love licking your hot little ass," I said.

We kissed for a while, and she rubbed my cock with her hand, trying to get me hard again. It wasn't long before I was hard, and I whispered in her ear that I wanted to fuck her up the ass.

"No, but you can stick your finger in there if you want," she said.

"Come on, let me fuck you in the ass; it's so much tighter," I said.

"Stop," she said, "not tonight."

I pushed my cock in her cunt and closed my eyes, enjoying the pure physical pleasure. I started fantasizing about Monica and imagined I was fucking her up the ass. Just as I was about to come, I said:

"Oh, Monica!"

Mary immediately slapped my face, and I lost my orgasm. She was furious. There was nothing I could say. Without uttering a word, she got dressed and stormed out. I had to laugh.

Chapter Twenty

The next morning, at school, I told Horace about it and he really howled.

"It's good for her," he said, "gives her something to think about."

"What if she breaks up with me?" I said.

"Are you kidding? Women love the competition. You couldn't get rid of Mary if you tried to," he said.

Just then, Mary walked into the café and ordered a cappuccino without looking at us. I told Horace not to laugh, but he didn't pay any attention to me.

"Mary!" Horace said loudly. "Come on over, sweetheart."

Mary looked at us with a mock-cruel face, and then broke out into a big smile. She came over to our table and sat down.

"I suppose he told you what he did last night," she said to Horace.

"Of course. Paul doesn't keep any secrets from me. It's no big deal, honey. I've done it myself hundreds of times!"

"I don't know which of you is worse," she said.

"You love us," he said.

"I guess I do, against my better judgment," she said with a grin.

Mary and I went to class, and I was relieved that she forgave me. Horace was right, of course. Mary wouldn't let me out of her sight. She became even more possessive than she was before, and I began to feel suffocated. She wanted to go to lunch with me and come over again for dinner, but I politely made excuses and freed myself up for the rest of the day.

After morning classes, Horace and I took off to explore the city, which meant looking for pretty women. We walked through narrow cobblestone streets all the way downtown to a popular café in Piazza Republica. The café was crowded, and Horace scoped out the scene to find a likely spot to pick up women. We waited for a table and stood at the bar, sipping cappuccinos.

"Mary is starting to drive me crazy," I said.

"You should break it off with her, and open yourself up to other opportunities," he said.

"But the sex is great," I said.

"That'll wear off after a while," he said.

"Victoria has been hitting on me lately," I said. "Maybe I should go out with her."

"Take every opportunity while you're single," he said.

"Look at those two who just walked in," I said.

Horace turned slowly to check out two gorgeous blondes who looked Swedish. They were about twenty years old and undoubtedly were in some school.

"Don't go over there right away," he said.

"I hope they speak English," I said.

The young women ordered their coffees and stood at the bar chatting. We were about ten feet away, with a few people between us. Just thinking about trying to pick them up made me feel guilty, but being with Horace, who validated our intent, made me willing to go along.

"Since you speak Italian, you're going to have to do all the talking," he said.

"All right. But how are we going to slip over there without

being too obvious?" I said.

"I'll go over behind them when the bartender moves down," he said.

After several minutes had passed, the bartender moved to the other end of the bar to take some orders, and Horace walked past the women to order another coffee. I waited a few minutes, and then casually walked down to join him. We were standing right behind them, and I was trying to think of something clever to say.

"Do you speak English?" I said to them.

"A little," one said with a warm smile.

When Horace heard that, he just took over. He asked them their names, and we introduced ourselves. One of the women had delicate features, and was about five foot eight in height. Her name was Uma, and her smile penetrated like a dagger. Her English was better than her friend's, whose name escaped me immediately.

"Are you in school here?" Horace said.

"Yes, we are learning Italian," Uma said.

"I'm studying with Syracuse University, from the States," I said.

"You are Americans, yes?" Uma's friend said.

"Yes," we answered together.

They couldn't understand a lot of what we said, but they knew we were interested in getting their phone number.

"We live on the other side of the river," I said.

Uma gave me their phone number; I was ready to end the conversation and call them some other time, but Horace wanted to set the hook deeper.

"What else are you studying?" he said.

"History of art," Uma's friend said.

Horace kept them chatting for a while. Then he gestured with his eyes that he wanted to leave. We said goodbye and walked out with wide smiles on our faces.

"That Uma likes you," Horace said.

"How do you know?" I said.

"She was avoiding your gaze the entire time," he said.

I laughed to myself. Horace was as smooth as could be. We went to the central market and bought our fresh vegetables and meat for the day.

"Don't call them right away," Horace advised. "Give them a few days to think about it."

After the market, we walked back to my apartment, where John and Jesse were studying. We decided to play some pitch and played for two or three hours as usual, until Melanie showed up with Mary. I was a little disgruntled that Mary appeared, but I settled down after a few minutes.

Following dinner, Mary and I went into my bedroom, where I decided to make a little speech.

"Mary, you're starting to suffocate me. You have to give me more space," I said.

Her face turned sad and worried, and she grew perfectly silent.

"I really care about you, but I need my independence," I added.

"I understand," she said finally, without looking at me.

We sat and talked for a while, and I kept reassuring her that I wasn't breaking up with her. At one point, I kissed her, and the next minute we were rolling around on the bed tearing our clothes off. She knew I liked to have my cock sucked, and she worked on it like never before, making a lot of noise and swallowing my come. There was nothing more pleasurable than coming in her mouth. She rubbed my balls for the next few minutes, until I got hard again.

"Fuck me in the ass," she whispered.

I rolled her over and reached for the Vaseline on the table next to the bed. I inserted one lubricated finger, and she groaned loudly. Just then, Horace walked up to the door and shouted:

"Cut it out in there!"

We laughed, and I slowly thrust my hard cock in her ass. She masturbated herself as I fucked her, and in a minute, she came with a violent orgasm.

"I'll give you another," I said.

I could last a long time the second time around, and I kept thrusting with all my might. As she began to orgasm the second time, I told her to slow down so that we could come together. She tried to slow down, and I tried to catch up, but she came again, and her entire body shook. She was exhausted and wanted me to pull out, so I masturbated kneeling over her and came on her face.

"How do I look?" she said.

"Sexy," I said.

After we rested, I wanted her to leave, but I didn't know how I would tell her. We took a shower together, and while we were bathing, I said:

"You don't mind if I sleep alone tonight, do you?"

"No, that's fine. I understand," she said.

I was relieved she took it so well and glad I had said something to her. Horace was still drinking with John after Mary left, and I decided to have a glass of wine before going to bed.

Chapter Twenty-One

In the morning I felt well rested and emotionally strong. I walked by the statue of David as usual, but didn't even notice it. I was becoming a citizen of Florence, and the novelty of the city was beginning to wear off. I was looking forward to seeing Monica. The memory of the previous night lingered in my mind. As usual, Horace was sitting in the café, sipping his cappuccino, waiting for me to arrive.

"So you kicked her out last night, huh?" he said.

"Not really, I just told her she needed to give me more space. She took it well," I said.

"Monica just went up to her studio," he said.

"I'm not chasing anybody any more. I want to do my own thing and hang out with the boys," I said.

Horace laughed.

"Sure, whatever, Paul," he said.

I went to class and actually paid attention for a change. We were discussing Romantic literature, and I was interested in de Man's theory that Wordsworth is just as modern as Yeats. If pure repetition is impossible, I guess every piece of work is new and unique every time it is read, no matter when it was written.

Mary wasn't in class, and I wondered where she was. Ellen was asking a lot of questions as usual and participating in class more than anyone else. I was listening to the discussion when George passed me a note.

"I want to fuck you," it said, and was signed, "Blondie."

Immediately, I looked at George. He nodded toward a girl named Christine who was sitting by the window. Christine had dark brown hair and was mostly Italian. She winked at me, and I got a big smile on my face. I wrote her a note saying, "anytime," and she nodded when she read it. I began scheming right away, trying to figure out how to do this without getting caught.

After class, I sat with Horace and showed him the note. He was amused by it and said, "Just hang out with the boys, huh?"

I laughed and shook my head.

"Should I take her up on it?" I asked.

"Of course," he said. "Listen, these girls have very few men to choose from, and they want to get laid while they're in Italy. You just happen to be the most available."

"What if Monica finds out?" I said.

"Fuck Monica. She's just playing you. She likes to pull your chain," he said.

I fantasized about Christine. She was very beautiful and very sexy, and I really wanted to fuck her. I knew she had her own apartment with another woman named Julia, and I thought maybe I would drop Mary in order to go out with Christine. While we were talking in the café, Christine walked in and stood at the bar.

"Make your move," Horace said.

I hesitated for a second, then walked up to her.

"What's going on?" I said.

"Nothing," she smiled.

"Were you serious?" I said.

"Of course," she said. "You seem surprised."

"Well, this is the first time anyone has approached me this way," I said.

"It might be the last time too," she said.

"Do you want to go to lunch or something?" I said.

"Sure," she said.

"I must admit I'm a little off balance," I laughed.

"Good," she said.

We went to a little trattoria down the street and sat by ourselves in a dark corner. She was as cool as a cucumber and didn't mention anything about sex. We ordered pasta and a glass of wine and talked about various people in the program. We knew each other a little bit, but had not talked about anything extensively. Christine had lovely, big brown eyes and I got hard just looking at her.

"Why don't I come over to your place and see your apartment?" I said.

"Good idea," she said.

I didn't know if I was really going to get laid, but it seemed like a real possibility. She was on the second floor of a fairly modern building, not far from the school. We sat in the living room, which was decorated with old furniture, and we talked about our pasts. Christine was from a very wealthy family in Connecticut, and had been raised with all the privileges money could buy. She had attended private schools all her life and had lost her virginity at a very early age. After a while, we brought the conversation up to the present.

"Why did you decide to approach me that way?" I said.

"I figured it would capture your attention," she said.

"You succeeded," I said.

I was sitting next to her, deciding on the right moment to kiss her. I held her hand for a minute, then pulled her toward me and gently pressed my lips against hers. She responded by opening her mouth and pushing her tongue against mine. I immediately got a hard on. She was a great kisser. She let me put my hand on her breast and, after a minute of rubbing, I put my hand under her shirt. She was moaning and groaning, so I put my hand between her legs and massaged her pussy. After I put her hand on my cock, she unbuttoned my pants and slid her hand under my shorts.

At this point, I thought for sure I was going to get laid, but I took my time and figured I would bring her to the brink of orgasm before I tried to pull her pants off. She sounded like she was in ecstasy, but you never know when a woman is faking it. I flicked my finger quickly over her clitoris, and suddenly she arched her back and said:

"I'm coming! Oh my God!"

At that point I tried to pull her pants off, but she stopped me.

"No, not yet," she said.

I was so frustrated, I said:

"You get to come, but I don't?"

"I'll jerk you off," she said.

"Why don't you blow me," I said.

"Next time," she said.

She managed my cock with her hand, but she couldn't bring me to orgasm, so I helped her out. I started jerking off right in front of her face, which got her really excited.

"I want to come in your mouth," I said.

She didn't say anything, but she didn't put her mouth on my cock, and I came all over her face. Suddenly, without warning, I thought of Mary and worried that she was going to find out. After I came, all I wanted to do was get out of there. She wanted to talk, but I made an excuse and tried to dress slowly, trying not to give myself away.

"Would you like to come over for dinner tomorrow night?" she asked.

"I'll call you," I said.

I felt a tremendous sense of relief as I stepped out into the street. All I could think was that Mary would find out and break up with me. I walked downtown feeling like I needed a cappuccino to settle down. In Italy I often felt that some of my best moments were when I was sitting alone sipping coffee.

I believed that my first novel would be about this year in Florence, and I would look around remembering certain spots in the city and the adventures I had had with my friends. With that in mind, I began keeping a journal, writing down conversations and outlining character descriptions. There was plenty of material, but I thought I couldn't write all the intimate sexual details. Later, I would change my mind about that. Why not describe my sexual exploits, which were fortunate and unusual due to the number of women in our program?

I sat in Piazza Republica, as cold as it was, and watched the passersby. I thought about Horace and the number of women he claimed to have fucked. I knew I was getting a reputation in school, but it didn't seem to bother the women. Then I thought that when Monica found out about this latest exploit, my chances with her would be even slimmer.

I walked home almost dejected, not knowing exactly why. I figured I would have to break up with Mary. It was only fear, and this feeling disturbed me. John was reading when I got home, and I was glad to see him, because I needed somebody to talk to.

"Hey, what's up?" I said.

"Nothing. What's wrong with you?" he said.

"I'm depressed. I just got a hand job," I said.

"Why is that depressing?" he laughed.

"I feel guilty."

"Here we go again," he said. "Who was it?"

"Christine. She sent me a note in class and, of course, I couldn't resist the temptation."

He shook his head.

"Most guys would be thrilled to have all the opportunities you have. Why do you feel so guilty?"

"Because I'm going out with Mary," I said.

"Mary probably loves the fact that you cheat on her. It makes you harder to get," he said.

"That's what Horace says," I said.

"You have other opportunities. Why don't you take advantage of them?" I said.

"I'm not interested," he said. "Lighten up. Christ, it's not like you have any real problems."

"You're right," I said, and felt better.

Then I told him my episode with Christine, and he couldn't stop laughing. He really burst out when I told him what she looked like with come all over her face and her surprised expression. My greatest asset has always been my sense of humor, and John loved to hear the way I told my stories. That night I went to sleep feeling like a stud, and as the various faces and pussies I had enjoyed passed through my mind, I masturbated myself into a deep sleep.

Chapter Twenty-Two

Christmas break was arriving very quickly, and I was sad to see most of the students leave, but I was glad my roommates and core of friends were going to stay. Mary had been planning to leave, but she was having such a good time, she decided to remain. In the back of my mind I had decided to break up with Mary, and I couldn't wait to see the new batch of students. I had a friend who lived in Birmingham, England; I was planning a long trip by train to visit him. I had been writing him letters. He was in school as well and had come to the States several years earlier to work in summer camp. His name was Roger, and I was anxious to see him. I was thinking of going with Mary, but I decided it would be easier to go alone.

Monica was going to Paris for the break. Her parents had friends there, and she was excited to see all the artwork. I wanted to ask her if I could go to Paris with her but chickened out. Horace and Melanie were going to Rome. Melanie was doing a project on churches and wanted to take a lot of pictures. John was going to Greece, and Jesse was going to Germany and Austria. Jesse was quite the independent traveler; even without any money, he could go just about anywhere and get by.

I took my guitar with me to England and spent the hours on the train practicing. The trip was tiring, but I was so glad to see Roger that I stayed up all night talking to him. Roger was three or four years older than I, and he was interested in literature as well. When we had worked at summer camp together, we used to exchange books and talk about them late into the night.

He was living with four other guys, and the house was in complete disarray. Beer was always in the house and, of course, we drank tea in the morning. Roger had a great sense of humor; we really got each other going. He loved the United States but thought that most Americans were ignorant, a common feeling for the Brits. After I slept the entire next day, I went with the five of them to their favorite pub; they were adamant about getting me drunk.

The pub was relatively new, and quite large. The interior was made of a rich old wood with a deep shine. Roger and I sat alone, while the other guys stood at the bar socializing with their friends. There were plenty of women, but that first night I wasn't paying any attention. Roger was seriously dating a woman named Sue and wasn't on the prowl like his roommates.

"What's Sue like?" I said, sipping a dark ale.

"She's hot." He laughed.

"Besides that," I said.

"She's very independent and assertive. I can't push her around," he said.

"You need that," I said.

"She's got short blonde hair, and a slinky body with big tits," he said.

"Sounds like marriage material," I said.

"We'll see, but I do love her," he said. "What about you?"

"I'm playing the field," I said.

"You should act your age," he said.

I looked over at the bar and saw his roommates hitting on some women. Their laughter was really loud; I loved the English sense of humor. It was much more sophisticated than ours and contained a great deal of bitter irony. Irony and laughter are soul mates. When separated from one another, they seem lost.

"I've got my eye on a girl named Monica, but so far she only wants to be friends," I said.

"What's she like?" he said.

"She's amazing, the most beautiful woman you've ever seen, with long blonde hair that she wears in a braid, and she's a very talented painter. Italian, of course," I said.

"Now that sounds like marriage material," he said.

"I'd marry her in a minute," I said. "The problem is she watches me fuck these other women and won't have anything to do with me."

"Keep in touch with her after you go back to the States. She may change her mind," he said.

"Meanwhile, I'm fucking this cute little Mary, who takes it up the ass," I said.

"That's disgusting," he laughed.

"Why is it disgusting?" I said.

"God never intended that orifice to be abused," he said.

"I don't believe in God; besides she likes it that way," I said.

He rolled his eyes and called me a pervert. I just shrugged my shoulders and laughed it off. One of Roger's friends, named Geremy, came over to our table and sat down. Naturally, the first words out of Roger's mouth were that I was fucking Mary up the ass.

"Good," Geremy said.

"See, Roger," I said.

Roger shook his head and snickered. We had a few more drinks. Then I told him we had to leave, because I was really tired. The next day, I woke up early. Snow was on the ground, and the sun was out. The boys were up already, drinking tea in the kitchen. Two young women were with them, whom I have never seen before. I was introduced and figured out by the conversation whom they had slept with. Roger had to go to work, so I was on my own.

    I took a bus to downtown Birmingham and found a nice coffee shop to hang out in. I was glad to have a cappuccino. The tea didn't thrill me. I had brought a book with me, and I buried my head in it. After reading for a while, a lovely woman asked if she could sit at my table, since there weren't any seats left. I thought this was my lucky day and invited her to join me. She got very excited when she found out I was American; there weren't too many tourists around. She was a little older than I and was a graduate student. Her name was Jenny. We got into a discussion about the Romantics and discovered that Wordsworth was our favorite writer. She was as passionate about literature as I was and could quote long passages of poetry. Finally, I asked her if she had a boyfriend.

    "Sort of, but not really," she said.

    "Well, I'm only here for two weeks. Would you like to get together sometime?"

    "Sure, I'd love to," she said.

We made a date for the next evening; we were going to meet at the same table at seven o'clock. I knew that we were merely meeting as friends, but it was a good way for me to get out of the house. She was there when I arrived and had a radiant smile on her face. She had brought some poetry that she had written, and I thoroughly enjoyed reading it. Actually, she was a pretty decent poet. I told her about my desire to write novels and ran a few ideas past her.

"What do you think about putting a lot of sex in a novel?" I asked.

"I think it's all right if it's relevant," she said. "What did you have in mind?"

"I want to write a novel about this year in Florence and, as it turns out, I'm having a lot more sex than usual, because there are so many women in our program," I said.

"Then you should," she said. "Besides, it won't hurt sales."

"Don't you think it would cheapen it?" I said.

"It depends on how you handle it. If it's true to your experience, you should write about it. D.H. Lawrence staked his entire reputation on opening up literature to such an exploration. Besides, people love reading about sex, whether they admit it or not," she said.

Jenny had blonde hair down to her shoulders, which glistened in the light, a very fair complexion, and deep blue eyes. I wanted to kiss her in the worst way. We really enjoyed each other's company; she was very curious about the States and wanted to know everything about America. I asked her if she wanted to go for a walk, thinking how at the right moment I would sneak a kiss. Downtown Birmingham wasn't very beautiful, but it didn't matter, we were too engrossed in conversation. She put her arm in mine as we walked. I felt like I had known her for a long time.

"What's your boyfriend like?" I asked her.

"I wouldn't really call him my boyfriend. We don't sleep together; we're just close friends," she said. "What's your girlfriend like?"

"She's lively, and smart, and sexy, but I think she's too inexperienced for me. I'm not in love with her. I like older women," I said, winking at her.

"We should keep in touch after you go back to the States," she said.

"I'll write you from Italy too. I love getting mail," I said.

I couldn't wait any longer. I stopped her and pulled her toward me gently, giving her a tender kiss on the lips. She put her arms around me and squeezed me tight, pushing her tongue deep inside my mouth. I was thinking of putting my hand between her legs, but I decided against it. Instead, I grabbed her ass, which she let me do. We were on a deserted side street, and the street lamp above her illuminated her gentle features. We kissed for a few minutes. Then she pushed me away with a shy look on her face.

"You're a good kisser," I said.

"So are you," she smiled.

We walked arm in arm for a few more blocks, then returned to the café. We made a date for several nights later.

I took the bus back out to the suburbs. It was cold in the house. The electric portable heaters hardly did the job. Roger was still up, and I told him about the date. He laughed when I told him we made out on a downtown street. I went to bed and read her poetry for a while. Even though it was very cold in the house, I had plenty of blankets and slept well.

Chapter Twenty-Three

For the next few days, I was pretty bored, because Roger and the boys had school or work, and I had little to do. I was looking forward to my date with Jenny, but the days dragged. Finally, the evening of our date arrived, and I was a little too excited. It never occurred to me that she might not show up. I had tried to write a poem and had brought it with me, hoping she would help me edit it. I got to the café twenty minutes early and tried to sip my cappuccino slowly. Then I worked on my poem, realizing I had no idea what I was doing. The time of our meeting passed, and she was nowhere to be seen. Each minute dragged by as I kept looking at my watch. I was about to leave when I saw her smiling face through the window. I was ecstatic.

"Hi. I thought you weren't going to show," I said.

"The bus was late; I'm glad you didn't leave," she said.

I noticed she had put makeup on, as she hadn't done before. She looked even better than the last time. I was a little nervous, probably because she was older and more experienced than the girls I had dated.

"I tried to write a poem, but I failed miserably. I thought you might help me with it," I said.

"I'm sure it's not as bad as you think. We're always our own worst critics. Let me see it," she said.

As I gave her the poem, which was scratched out all over the place, I suddenly felt very vulnerable. I watched her face closely, looking for clues, but I noticed no change. After she finished, she read it again.

"You have potential!" she said.

"That means it sucks," I said.

"No, not at all. You use too much alliteration, but your theme is great," she said.

She took her pen and did some quick work on it. When she showed it to me I didn't even recognize the poem, but it had been improved considerably. It was my first creative writing lesson, and I believed that I had potential.

"Did you notice the sexual metaphors?" I asked.

"Of course." She smiled. "Are you obsessed with sex, or does it just come naturally?" she laughed.

"I'm limited in my depth," I said.

We went for a walk again, but I wasn't thinking about grabbing her; I was daydreaming about becoming a famous poet. We walked arm in arm, and for the first time in my life, I realized that I had to marry a writer. It was cold. She held me very closely, and as always, I imagined myself married to her. We walked to the same spot as before and immediately kissed each other passionately. I was a little braver that evening and slipped my hand between her legs, which surprisingly, she let me do. Suddenly, I felt her hand on my cock and was ready to fuck her right there.

I unzipped my pants and stuck her hand inside. A little sperm was oozing out, and she was getting very wet.

"Why don't you come back to the house, and we'll make love?" I said.

"No, you're leaving in a few days. I don't want to just fuck and then say goodbye," she said.

Instead of trying to persuade her any further, I concentrated on bringing her to orgasm, which I hoped might change her mind. We were in an unlit alley, but I kept looking out to the street to see if anyone was watching. I was so excited I thrust my tongue deep in her mouth, and she sucked on it.

"We can't do this," she said, as I pushed two fingers up her cunt.

"I can't stop," I said.

"Let's go to your house," she said.

"No, let's fuck right here," I said.

She groaned in ecstasy as I rubbed her clit. I wanted her to suck my cock, but I didn't think she would. I tried pulling her pants down, but it was very difficult.

"Suck me," I said.

She immediately got on her knees in the wet street and stuck my cock in her mouth. She was talented at the art; I came after a minute, gushing sperm into her hungry mouth. She swallowed it down and laughed a deep laugh afterwards. We quickly got dressed and sauntered out into the quiet street as if we had just been strolling.

"I'm surprised you went so far," I said.

"Why is it that men can go as far and as fast as they want, but women are supposed to show restraint?" she said.

"No reason, I guess. That's the way we're socialized."

"Well, it sucks," she said. "Men can sleep with as many women as they want, but if a woman sleeps around, she's considered a slut!"

"It's not as bad as it used to be," I said. "Besides, men are considered sluts too if they aren't choosy about who they sleep with."

"It's not fair," she said.

"Nothing about life is fair," I countered.

We walked back into the café and ordered another drink.

"You're not feeling guilty about what we did, are you?" I said.

"No, not at all," she said. "Why do you say that?"

"Well, you reacted pretty strongly."

She sat silently for a minute, thinking about what I had said. There is an echo for every word and action we speak or take, and the echo of our lovemaking was tainted by the echo of our discussion afterwards. I felt stupid for saying what I had said, destroying a beautiful moment and making her feel bad for expressing her passion. I was determined to reverse my stupidity.

"Listen, I'm flattered that you wanted to make love to me. I wasn't questioning your motives. I would have never pushed you if I hadn't wanted you," I said.

"Never mind," she said.

"No, I shouldn't have said what I said, and I apologize. I really like you, you're a great person."

She smiled, which made me feel better, but the moment of ecstasy had been lost, and it would have taken a long time to engender another. She was tough though, and our conversation regained a tone of respect and intimacy. The problem was that we didn't have enough time to establish a friendship.

"This experience could turn into a poem," I said.

"Easily," she laughed.

Her laughter was delightful. Like birds singing to each other, we lightened our discussion and our laughter blended in midair. I teased her about our lovemaking, trying to restore our sexual moment to its original beauty.

"Where did you learn to give such great blow jobs?" I said.

"I got my skills from a book," she said.

"You'll have to lend me that book. I know a couple of

women who should read it," I said.

It was getting late, but neither of us wanted to leave. I could see she had gotten over her distress and was feeling better. As she was sipping her coffee, I imagined my sperm gushing into her mouth. I couldn't help these sexual thoughts. Her beauty triggered them.

"Why don't you come over to our house tomorrow night?" I said.

Suddenly, she grew serious, but I didn't know why.

"I don't think so; I don't want to get involved. It'll be harder for me when you leave," she said.

I felt sad and wished that she could come back to Italy with me. We made a date for the next night, but I knew I wouldn't show and figured she wouldn't either. I gave her a kiss goodnight and went to wait for the bus.

Chapter Twenty-Four

Roger and I spent the weekend together, laughing the whole time, as we reminisced about our experience at summer camp. At the end of two weeks, I was sad to leave, but excited about returning to Florence and seeing my friends. The train ride back was exhausting. I don't think I slept at all. When Florence came into sight, I felt like I was home. I knew each church spire that reached to the sky; there are few cityscapes that are as stunning. I was looking forward to seeing John and Jesse, but nobody was home when I arrived. When I called Mary's house, I was pleased that she answered.

"Hi, sweetheart. How was your trip?" I said.

"Absolutely fabulous. I wish you had been with me," she said.

"My trip was great too, but I didn't get much sleep. I'm exhausted," I said.

"I slept a long time after I arrived yesterday," she said. "Why don't you go to bed and call me later?"

After looking around the apartment for signs of life, I went to bed. Jesse's bed wasn't made, but John's was, so I figured Jesse was home. I fell into a deep sleep at about four in the afternoon and didn't awaken until the next morning. It was Sunday; the city was alive with church bells, and the sun was shining. I woke up with a hard on, and I laughed to myself when I thought I looked like a miniature statue of David. I felt refreshed, jumped out of bed, and went out for a jog. The streets were empty, and the air was crisp. I felt out of shape, and after two miles, I started walking. I stopped at the bar on the corner and ordered my usual cappuccino. Sitting quietly by myself, I listened to the men who frequented the bar.

They were workers and members of the communist party, which was quite popular in Italy. They were complaining about everything. I was learning that in Italy, politics is much more complicated and confusing than it is in the States. Italians argue and fight about everything and little gets done. It seemed to me that they were about fifty years behind us and in a hurry to catch up.

When I got home, I called Horace and Melanie, and Horace answered in a very sleepy voice.

"Get up, you lazy bum!" I said.

"We got in at about four in the morning. Give me a break," he said.

"Did you have a good time?" I asked.

"Great time, but let me go back to sleep. I'll call you later," he said.

I called Mary and made a date to shop at the food market downtown. We met at a little café and had a cappuccino before going shopping. I was delighted to see her. We decided to have a big dinner at our apartment and bought all kinds of food. It was great to be in Florence again; just the air and the architecture made me feel inspired. When we got back to the apartment, we jumped right into bed and fucked our brains out. I loved coming in her mouth and watching her swallow it. Afterwards, we napped and then called everybody for our big dinner.

Horace was in a great mood when he arrived. He began cooking right away, singing like an Italian opera star. Melanie and Mary sat in the living room looking at pictures from their trip, while Jesse and I helped Horace. Of course, I invited Monica. She showed up a little later with tight stretch pants that drove me crazy. She was in the kitchen bending over the sink, and I was staring at her ass, when Horace held a carrot behind her like a big dildo. I laughed so hard that Monica turned around and gave Horace a dirty but smiling look. We were all glad to be reunited, and the wine started flowing.

"A toast, a toast," Horace yelled, "to the world travelers gathered in Florence, the greatest city every built."

Everybody told stories of their adventures, but I left out the most interesting part of my trip. The women were drunk in no time; none of them could hold their liquor since they rarely drank. Monica talked about Paris as if there were no more interesting places on earth.

"One night I was at an American bar, when this handsome Frenchman came up to me and introduced himself," she said.

"I bet his name was Pierre," Horace said.

"No, his name was Jacques, and he was a graduate student. He was a little short, naturally, but cute as could be," she said.

"He told you his father was a great painter and wanted to bring you back to his studio to see the work," Horace said.

"Not exactly, but close," Monica said. "He is a writer and wanted to take me back to his place to read poetry to me."

"And you went, of course," I said.

"Not exactly, but close," she said. "I told him I would walk down the avenue with him, and he could recite one of his poems."

"Then he fucked you in a dark alley," Horace said.

"Not exactly," she said. "We walked along the river's edge, and he kissed me in a very tender way. Then, believe it or not,

147

he proposed to me!"

"You fool," Horace yelled. "He was just trying to get in your pants."

"I know. I wasn't born yesterday," she said.

"So, what happened?" Melanie said.

"That was it. We walked back and I left," Monica said.

"What a terrible ending to a possibly exciting story," Horace said.

I was so jealous I didn't believe a word of her story. I was certain she had gone back to his place and fucked him to death. We got out the cards and played poker late into the night, joking and carrying on. Mary spent the night; we made love for an hour, experimenting a little bit, and ended with me squirting my load into her mouth.

"I love you," she said.

"I love you too," I said.

The next morning we got up early. I was anxious to see the new batch of students at school. We stood outside the villa, waiting for the bus to arrive. Mary was standing very close to me. She wasn't going to let me out of her sight, and she was claiming her territory. It was amazing. One gorgeous woman after another stepped off the bus as if it were a beauty pageant.

One on particular caught my attention. She had short blonde hair and sparking blue eyes. Her smile made my heart jump. She possessed a regal walk that made it seem as though she was floating through air. We followed them inside, and the twelve of us who had remained from the previous semester introduced ourselves. Her name was Jennifer. For the first time that year, someone took my mind off of Monica. I played it cool, making a conscious effort not to stare. The families hosting the students arrived a little later, and soon everyone had left the school.

John was sleeping when I got home. I was anxious to hear of his adventures. I went to bed and took a long nap. I was still catching up on my sleep. At about five, I got up, and John was cooking away, whistling and singing to himself.

"You're in an unusually good mood. You must have had a hell of a trip," I said.

"It was spectacular. Wait until you see my pictures. I met a woman too!" he said.

"Oh, oh, now you're in trouble," I said. "Patricia will be furious."

"Not if you don't tell her," he smiled.

"I'm afraid I've been a bad influence on you," I said.

"She's coming to Florence in a couple of months. We'll have to be very discreet," he said.

I laughed to myself, thinking that John too was susceptible to a wandering eye.

"I saw a beautiful new student this morning. She is so hot. I think I'm going to drop Mary," I said.

"Mary's going to be pissed and heartbroken at the same time," he said.

"I can't help it," I said, feeling a little guilty.

We ate dinner while John told me all about his adventures. What I was really interested in was whether he had fucked this woman or not.

"Did you, or did you not fuck her?" I pressed him.

"Of course I fucked her," he said.

"Was she good?" I said.

"Unbelievable," he said.

"Does she take it up the ass?" I said.

"No, of course not. You're fascinated with that aren't you? Most women don't, for your information. Your Mary is the exception to the rule."

I imagined fucking Jennifer up the ass, but for some reason I couldn't fantasize about that with Monica.

"What are you going to do with Patricia when this woman shows up?" I said.

"I don't know, but I can't have her stay here; I'll have to find a cheap pensione nearby where I can sneak over," he said.

"The plot thickens," I said.

John wanted a detailed description of all the new students and was pleased to find out that there were at least a dozen lovely girls ready for the taking. I decided to call Mary that night. I wasn't going to wait, and I was a coward, so I figured I would break up with her over the phone. I asked John what I should say to her, but he offered me no advice. My heart was racing as I dialed the number, and I had to sit down because my knees were shaking.

"Hello?" she answered.

"Hi, it's me," I said.

"Hi, sweetie. I was thinking about you," she said.

"What's going on," I said.

"Nothing. I was hoping you'd invite me over to spend the night," she said.

"Listen, Mary, we have to talk," I said.

"That doesn't sound good," she said.

"I don't know how to tell you this," I said.

"You're breaking up with me," she said.

"I'm sorry, sweetheart. I really love you, but I have to feel free over here," I said.

Then she started screaming.

"You just want to fuck those new girls!" she yelled.

I didn't know what to say, so I didn't say anything and just let her get it out. After a few minutes, she stopped and slammed down the phone. John was in the room and had heard everything she had said.

"That didn't go very well," I said.

"It never does," he said. "At least it's over with. Now you're a free man."

"It's going to be uncomfortable facing her in school," I said.

"She'll get over it," he said.

The echo of that phone call rang in my ears the rest of the evening, and it took me a long time to fall asleep. John had gone to bed early. The apartment was perfectly quiet, and I sat by my window looking out at the night lights. I hadn't wanted to hurt Mary's feelings, but there was no way around it. I thought about the new students I was going to meet, and I fantasized a little about Jennifer. When I finally put my head on the pillow, thousands of thoughts raced through my mind, and I had to count sheep over and over again to relax.

Chapter Twenty-Five

Even though I was not well rested the next morning, I got up early and went for a jog. The sun was up, but it was pretty cold. The fresh air woke me up, and the hills surrounding Florence seemed to be on fire. I stopped by our local café on the way back to the apartment and ordered a cappuccino. All the old men were there already, talking and laughing; the vitality of the city ran through their veins. John and Jesse were awake when I got back, and a half hour later the three of us took the bus to school. All we talked about was our new classes, and the women we were going to meet.

The car was full, but Horace was saving me a seat. He was already wound up from drinking a few cups of coffee.

"Hey, Paolo. What's going on?" he yelled over the buzz.

"I broke up with Mary," I told him quietly.

"Good timing," he said wryly.

As I sat there talking to Horace, I noticed all the new women checking me out. I pretended not to be aware of them and sipped my cappuccino. Jennifer was not there, but I saw a dark haired beauty who kept looking over at me. Horace was teasing the hell out of me, which really made me laugh.

"You've got to number them and keep them in order. It could get to be very confusing," he said.

"I'm just going for one," I said seriously.

"Sure, whatever," he said.

The dark haired girl had the sweetest heart shaped ass and

showed it off with her tight jeans. As I was staring at her ass, Jennifer walked in. Her blonde hair was pulled back, and she had just a little bit of makeup on. She was wearing jeans too, and I got a look at her pert little ass and skinny legs.

"I like that one," I said to Horace.

"She's hot," he said.

Then Monica came in with her hair in a braid, wearing a beautiful dress.

"This is too much to take," I said.

"Keep your cool," Horace said.

Classes began a little later. My first class was Modern English Literature, which I loved. Jennifer was in this class as well, along with many of the other new students. I sat a few seats behind Jennifer so I could stare at her hair and fantasize about grabbing it as I fucked her from behind. Following class, we all went back into the café, but this time I stood at the bar to make myself available to meet the girls. Horace joined me, and pretty soon we were engaged in a conversation with Stephanie, who was a cute little blonde from Syracuse, New York, my hometown. Horace was dominating the conversation, as usual, so I sat back and played it cool.

"Paul lives on the other side of the river, with John and Jesse, and they have the best parties," he said.

"Horace cooks at our apartment all the time," I said.

"What places do you go to at night?" she said.

"There are a few of places that have dancing, but it's not like the States. We just hang out at Paul's place most of the time," Horace said.

Stephanie was very petite, with a cute little ass, which she stuck out as she leaned against the bar. She was very fuckable, but I was after Jennifer, who seemed to be playing it very cool.

"Why don't you come to our apartment tonight and have dinner with us?" I said.

"I'd love to," she said.

Later, Horace and I went to the market to buy food for dinner. We bought two bottles of '64 Chianti, which turned out to be a very delicious wine. We decided to have fried chicken again, Horace's specialty, with pasta and broccoli.

"Why did you invite Stephanie to dinner if you're interested in Jennifer?" Horace said on our way home.

"She's a decoy," I said, grinning. "No, I'm just kidding. I think she's nice. Why not give her a taste of our hospitality? Plus she's from Syracuse. I may be friends with her back home."

"I'll bet you'll give her a taste of your hospitality," he laughed.

John was home when we arrived. The three of us played cards until five, when we started cooking. Stephanie showed up with her roommate Melissa, who was a cute little blonde too. Melanie was a bit late, but we had saved her some food. After dinner, the wine began to flow, and soon we were laughing at everything, whether it was funny or not. Horace wanted to play strip poker, but the women didn't want to. It turned out that Stephanie had a pretty sharp wit and was able to defend herself well against a barrage of sexual innuendos leveled against her by Horace. Melissa was quieter, and after a few drinks had a little smile on her face.

"Are you two looking for Italian men, like the rest of the women?" Horace said.

"I think they're looking for us," Stephanie said. "I've been pinched twice already."

"They love American blondes," John said.

"They're so forward. They'll say anything. They don't care," Stephanie said.

"They're just playing," I said.

"I think I prefer American men," Stephanie said.

"Don't judge so quickly," I said. "There are some Italian men who are very well educated, very artistic, with a wonderful sense of humor. This is quite a different culture. You might want to date an Italian man just for a unique experience."

Stephanie got up to go the bathroom. Her very tight jeans outlined her sexy little ass. Horace noticed me staring and winked at me. I looked at Melissa, who was quietly drinking, being merely content to be there, a part of the gang. When Stephanie came back, I took a quick look at her crotch, which stuck out a little in those jeans. I hadn't really thought about fucking her until I had seen her walking toward me with a wiggle.

"Paul can't take his eyes off of you," Horace said.

"I think he's cute too," Stephanie said.

"He's a free man now," Horace said.

"You were going out with somebody last semester?" Stephanie said to me.

"Yeah, I was going out with Mary, but we recently broke up," I said.

"How did she take it?" she said.

"Pretty well, I guess. We had only been going out for a couple of months," I said.

I was staring at her tits while I was talking to her, because they were a good size and very bouncy. I was trying to think of a way to get her alone, but no opportunities were presenting themselves.

"Who wants more wine?" Horace said.

We were starting to run low on wine, and Horace wasn't slowing down at all. I was feeling pretty drunk and very horny, so at one point I put my foot between Stephanie's legs underneath the table. I was surprised that she let me keep it there, and I began rubbing her cunt with my toes.

"Are you going out with anyone, John?" Melissa asked.

"Yes. Her name is Patricia, but I don't know how long it's going to last," he said.

"Are there any Italian men hanging around the school, or going out with any of the girls?" Stephanie said.

"Some of the women were dating Italian men, but we don't see them very much," Horace said.

After a few minutes, Stephanie pushed my foot away, and my cock lost its erection. John went out with Melissa to buy more wine, as Horace polished off the last bottle. I asked Stephanie if she wanted to see my photographs of Sicily, and she agreed. We sat on my bed, very close together, as I narrated the story of our trip. After about twenty pictures, Stephanie leaned over and kissed me.

"I really like you," she said.

"I like you too," I said.

We kissed passionately, and I rubbed her breasts, which were so firm. She groaned in ecstasy, but she wouldn't let me put my hand down her pants. I got on top of her and dry fucked her, as she thrust her tongue deep inside my mouth. I unzipped my pants and pulled my cock out, and placed her hand on it. At first, she pulled back, but then she began to massage me. Apparently, Horace became impatient waiting for us, and at one point he yelled out:

"Hey, cut it out you two. This is a party. Get your asses out here!"

We laughed and kept kissing for a while. Then Stephanie pushed me away.

"We'd better go back out there," she said.

"Sure," I said, feeling pretty drunk.

Everybody stayed up for a while except me. I went to bed and passed out. In the morning, I woke up early, but fortunately, without a headache. I made myself a cappuccino, and wrote in my journal. I thought about Stephanie and realized that I had better cool it or I would be involved in another relationship that would be difficult to get out of.

I loved the mornings in Florence; sunny or not, the city was beautiful in its quiet splendor. When the sun peeked from the horizon, the rooftops blazed, and the birds sang with joy. I walked to the café on the corner where the early risers were already having their coffee and discussing current events. They loved to mock their politicians and always put tragedy in the context of comedy. When I got back to the apartment, John and Jesse were up, drinking coffee.

"You and Stephanie were going at it last night," John said.

"A little bit, but I don't think it'll happen again," I said.

The three of us took the bus to school. The café was already full and buzzing with excitement. Horace was sitting with Monica, and my heart leapt, thinking that he had already told her about Stephanie. He had a big grin on his face, and waved me over to my usual seat.

"Don't you ever get a hangover?" I said.

"Christ, I didn't drink enough to give a dog a hangover," he said.

"What about you?" Monica said.

"I'm dragging a little," I said.

"Sounds like you had a good time last night," she said.

Horace just laughed. After a few minutes Monica went up to her studio, and I noticed Jennifer hanging out with a girlfriend. I was angry with Horace.

"What did you say to Monica?" I asked.

"Nothing, nothing. I just told her you and Stephanie have a crush on each other," he said.

"Listen, Horace, don't say anything to anybody. Do you hear me? Monica already thinks I'm a slut. You're making my reputation worse," I said sternly.

"Oh, I'm sorry, but Monica isn't going to fool with you anyway," he said.

"I know, but what about the other girls. Did you ever think about that?" I said.

"All right, cool off. I promise to keep my mouth shut from now on," he said.

Chapter Twenty-Six

I never stayed angry long. By the afternoon, Horace and I were taking our customary walk to the market, laughing our asses off. We loved talking about sex.

"I asked Melanie to stick her finger up my ass last night while I jerked off in her mouth!" he said.

"That's all I needed to hear," I said. "Does she take it up the ass?"

"No. She's a conservative girl. She doesn't do anything kinky at all, which is why I love fucking her so much. With her it's like fucking a virgin every time," he said. "I like talking dirty to her, because I know it shocks her. She loves it, of course, but she never talks dirty herself."

"I like the nasty girls," I said, "the ones who fantasize about dick all day and yell: 'give it to me; fuck me harder.' Those girls make me hard as a rock."

He was practically snorting with laughter and I kept him going with even more ridiculous sexual situations.

"That's what you say, but in reality you only go out with the good, high class girls," he said.

"A lot of those girls have very dirty thoughts," I said. "I never heard anything like fuck me in the ass before; I was shocked at that."

"That's nothing," he said. "Wait till you run into a woman who's into bondage and sadomasochism."

"I doubt that'll ever happen," I said. "Did you get into

that?"

"No, not really, but I've heard some good stories," he said.

We arrived at the market, which was very crowded. The sun was out, and everybody was talking loudly and even shouting, trying to get what they needed. We went to our usual spots where the vendors recognized us, and Horace told me what to order. Horace had excellent taste, and we always got something special like a rare cheese or wine.

When we arrived at my place, we played cards with John and Jesse, talking about all the new students. There were many afternoons when the four of us hung out together, playing cards and talking. The lifestyle of the Italians would stick with me. I enjoyed not working too hard and spending time with my friends. I noticed a vast difference between the Italians and the Americans, no matter what country the Americans originally came from.

The long history of art at the center of Italian culture has given them a different appreciation of life and reality. Work is not the most important activity of life and, in fact, it usually falls far down on the list of priorities. Relationships form the cornerstone of their culture, and conversation is truly an art there. Most Italians can easily spend an entire day talking, joking, and eating, without being too worried about the next car they are going to buy.

Jesse didn't talk about women like we did the first month, but then he loosened up and learned how to laugh. Horace said that Jesse was so serious, he would marry a quiet intellectual and never experience good sex. Jesse, though, was experiencing great sex in Italy, and it was making his whole personality blossom. John, being from New York City, had heard it all, and laughed easily.

We began cooking early, and Horace talked constantly as he cooked, sipping wine like the galloping gourmet.

"Hey, are there any women coming over tonight?" Horace said.

"I don't know," John said, "but you'd better cook for an army. Who knows who'll show up?"

Sure enough, a few of our friends showed up with Melanie. Monica, Patricia, Melissa, and Stephanie all stomped in giggling and carrying on.

"What's so funny?" Horace said.

"You guys!" Monica said.

"We're not funny!" Horace said.

"Wanna bet?" she said.

"Here we are slaving over a hot stove, cooking for you, and all you can do is make fun of us," Horace said with mock hurt.

"Poor baby," Monica teased, "if it weren't for Melanie, you wouldn't even be here."

"That's funny," John said. "We were laughing at you too, particularly your lovemaking."

"Oh, now it's getting personal," Monica said. "Well, have you noticed that I don't even get near you guys?"

"Paul has noticed," Horace said.

"She's afraid of getting involved in something she can't control," I retorted.

The food was ready, and we all sat down to eat, somewhat crowded around our small dining room table. The conversation started out on the light side, talking about Italy, and laughing lovingly at the Italians. Then, as sometimes occurred, the conversation turned philosophical.

"Do you think most Italians are really Catholic and believe

in God?" Stephanie asked.

"Some do, some don't, but the Italians have a sense of humor about religion, which most cultures don't have," I said. "Boccacio, for example, as early as the Renaissance, loved to ridicule priests. Most Italians think it's perverse to live a celibate life, no matter what the reason might be," I said.

"I agree!" Horace shouted.

"I grew up in Italy and went to Catholic school," I explained. "The nuns were abusive and spent a great deal of time trying to instill fear and guilt."

"Wonderful!" Stephanie said sarcastically.

"I always found it interesting that they never felt guilty about indoctrinating children and confusing them with various fears, paralyzing them for life," I said.

"That's what's great about the States," John said. "Separation of church and state, including public schools, has been the most liberating structure ever invented. Even though our schools don't teach anything at all, it's probably to the benefit of people who eventually want to think for themselves," he added.

"That's the most positive spin I've ever heard on our worthless educational system!" I observed.

The wine was flowing, and Horace was fascinated with the discussion, since he was extremely intelligent but was not used to being around intelligent conversation.

"I'm atheist," I confessed. "I don't condemn religion or the belief in God, but I don't completely accept it either."

"I'm atheist too," Stephanie said.

"We're in the minority," I said.

"There are plenty of atheists in the Soviet Union," John said.

"What do you think of deconstruction?" Stephanie asked.

"Don't get him started," Jesse said.

It was too late to hold me back. This was one of my favorite topics of conversation.

"It's interesting, but it's not as great as some people seem to believe," I said.

"Why not?" Stephanie asked.

"First of all, it's easy to criticize someone else's work; I don't pretend to offer anything better and, of course, like all works it has its value," I said.

"You sound like you know all about it," Stephanie said.

"Well, one of my professors knows all about it, and he clued me in," I said.

"All right, let's hear it," Jesse said.

"It's a type of skepticism that says language is inadequate in conveying complete meaning. Of course, it depends on which Deconstructionist we're talking about. They all have different versions, and some contradict each other."

"Make this short," Horace said. "We don't have all night."

"I'll just talk about one issue, the big one, the existence of God," I said.

"Derrida is an atheist, isn't he?" Stephanie said.

"I think they all are, but it's difficult to say. They don't have the balls to come right out and say it like Nietzsche," I said. "Derrida calls his work an 'anti-theology,' which leads me to believe he's atheist. But here's my point. A skeptic, in order to be logically consistent, would have to be agnostic, not knowing whether God existed or not. How can a skeptic say, 'I know God doesn't exist'?"

"Interesting," Stephanie said.

Just then I felt Stephanie's hand on my lap squeezing my

cock gently. I got hard immediately, and it was difficult for me to continue.

"How can you be sure God doesn't exist?" Melanie said.

"From the argument of evil, and all of our scientific knowledge, plus the fact that I don't perceive God," I said. "The question is: What does this word 'know' mean, and how does it mean, or what are its effects?"

Stephanie slowly pulled down my zipper as I was talking and grabbed my firm dick. Everybody was so drunk they didn't even notice. After a few minutes, I came right in her hand and started laughing. Everybody looked at me in surprise.

"What's so funny?" John said.

"I was thinking of Woody Allen's line: What does a blow job mean in the age of deconstruction?"

"I think President Clinton must be a deconstructionist, because he thinks a blow job doesn't constitute sex!" John said.

Everybody roared as I watched Stephanie pull her hand up and lick my come off her fingers.

"But let's get back to your argument. What does the word know mean?" Monica asked.

"I'm not sure," I said, "but it seems to me it has to do with the interaction of memory and the present and, to an extent, the future, every time I ask myself the question: Does God exist? I say no. I know God doesn't exist, and it doesn't matter what the definition of God is, or the word exist."

"But what about somebody who says: I know God exists," Monica said.

"I say they're wrong," I said, "and they're sure I'm wrong. One of us has to be right, and the other one wrong. There's nothing in between."

"Why doesn't it matter how one defines God or existence?"

Stephanie said.

"It doesn't matter because the definitions will necessarily change every time, which might be one of the meanings of difference," I said. "Even Barbara Johnson doesn't understand Derrida. She can't decide whether Locan and Derrida are saying the same thing, and then concludes that decidability is undecidable, which, of course, is ridiculous. Since time and space are in constant motion, and two things, like words, cannot occupy the same space at the same time, pure repetition is impossible. First of all, one cannot reduce all of one's work to a statement like 'the sign is empty,' and then conclude two writers are saying the same thing. No two writers can say the same thing because every word takes on a different meaning for each writer, and words are transforming themselves every second, which explains why the past can never be repeated exactly."

"I'm totally confused now," said Monica.

"Everything, including language, is in flux or motion, and there's no going back. We are constantly changing, and the past is forever lost, except in memory and history," I said. "Because we are in motion, memory and history are in motion too, so there is no stable fact, or past present."

Having said that, I slipped my hand between Stephanie's legs, and I could feel the warm moisture.

"Nothing is immutable, and everything is unique. Even one writer cannot say the same thing twice, because his text exists in a different place or in a different time, or both," I said.

"What does this have to do with sex? I want to know," said Horace.

"You can never get the same blow job twice!" John laughed.

"Do you mean that if you copied something in a copier and

had exactly the same words on two pages, they would be different?" Monica said.

"Exactly! Now you're getting it," I said.

"You're saying that if you hand out the 'same' poem to everybody in the class, they all have a different text?" John said.

"That's exactly right," I said.

"Cool," Stephanie said.

I unzipped Stephanie's pants and slid my hand under her panties. She was so wet.

"Each word takes effect in its own space at its own time, whether it is read, written, spoken or thought," I said. "The effects of a word can never be repeated twice exactly."

"Then how is anything decidable?" Monica said.

"Well, everything is decidable at every moment, but it is reviewed afterwards. For example, I've decided that Barbara Johnson is wrong, but I might change my mind later. I've decided bad doesn't exist, and I don't believe I'll ever change my mind about that," I said. "We have to make decisions. We don't have any choice there."

Stephanie spread her legs, trying to pretend she was still involved in the conversation. I poured her another glass of wine and thought Plato would have enjoyed being at this dinner. Stephanie reached down between her legs and forced two of my fingers in her cunt. I was losing my train of thought.

"So has Derrida really made any advance in thought?" John said.

"Philosophers are always the last to discover things. Art deconstructed itself a long time ago, and even recently in the book *Steppenwolf,* one can see the binary between half man, half wolf deconstructed into infinite personalities," I said.

"That's me," Horace said, "half man, half wolf."

"To fiction writers in particular, a lot of these ideas are obvious, and fairly straightforward. Leave it to anal philosophers to use big words and confuse everybody," I said.

Stephanie started to moan right in front of everybody, so I removed my hand.

"Just remember my professor's formula: pure repetition is impossible because the original and the 'copy' cannot correspond in time and space. Everything is body; metaphysics and physics are bound together. There is no idea without an image or word or sound attached to it," I said.

"I'll forget all of it tomorrow!" Horace said.

"Excuse us," I said, as I grabbed Stephanie's hand and practically dragged her into the bedroom. I didn't care what Monica thought at that point. All that was on my mind was eating Stephanie's pussy. Everybody snickered when we exited into the bedroom, and I knew Horace was glad the philosophy lecture was over. We were pretty drunk, and we ripped each other clothes off, hungry to dive into bed.

Because we were drunk, we didn't take our time and caress each other slowly, teasing the body with gentle kisses. We dove into oral sex with me lying on my back and her sitting on my face. She had a beautiful blonde pussy, and I was shocked to discover she had a long clitoris, something I had never seen before. It must have been two inches long, and I sucked hard on it like a lollipop, until she came violently all over my face. It took her a little while to get me hard, and I had to teach her how to suck me properly.

"Press your tongue firmly against the shaft and suck hard like you're trying to pull the head off," I said.

"How's this?" she said.

"Press even harder with your tongue." I said.

She was a quick learner. My cock got hard as a rock, and it tingled all over. It took a long time for me to come, and she was startled with how much sperm squirted into her mouth. She gagged a little and spit it out all over my stomach. Then she said:

"I can usually swallow it, but there was too much of it."

She laughed, and so did I. Then she tried to kiss me, but the come on her lips made me push her away.

"You really know how to boost a guy's ego," I said.

"That's my job," she said.

"Do you want to spend the night?" I said.

"No, not tonight. Let's go out and join the party," she said.

We got cleaned up and went to join the others with big smiles on our faces. They all raised their glasses and cheered.

"How was it?" Horace yelled. "The girls say he's really well endowed!"

"I've seen bigger!" Stephanie laughed.

I noticed Monica wasn't very amused, but she didn't say anything. I knew she was jealous, but I was sure she believed that as long as she wasn't involved physically, she somehow was emotionally safe. An hour later, everybody left, and I collapsed with fatigue. I slept well and woke up with a hard on, which made me very happy.

Chapter Twenty-Seven

That morning, as I walked to school, I knew that Stephanie and I would be a popular topic of conversation amongst my friends. Horace was talking to Monica in the café, and I felt slightly uncomfortable sitting at our table.

"There he is!" Horace said, letting me know they were talking about me.

"Hello, Studley," Monica said.

"Give me a break," I said.

"The women have taken numbers. You might want to find out what your schedule is for the semester," she said.

"You're just jealous because you're not getting any," I said.

"How do you know that? I wouldn't presume if I were you," she said.

Horace had a leering look on his face. He was enjoying himself immensely.

"You know you want him, Monica," Horace said.

"I could have him if I wanted him." She smiled.

"Not any more," I said.

"He's easy. He's a slut!" she said.

"Every good man is a slut, until they settle down," Horace said.

"Easy to get, hard to keep," I said.

Stephanie strolled in with a huge smile on her face, and Horace motioned her to join us. She had stretch pants on, which outlined every curve of her ass and crotch.

"Good morning!" she chirped.

"Sleep well?" Horace said.

"Like a baby," she said.

"There's nothing like a good roll in the hay to make one sleep well!" Horace said.

"Keep it down," I said.

"Don't worry, Paul. Everyone knows already," Monica said.

I just shook my head.

"I need a model. Do you want to sit for me?" Monica asked me.

"Sure, but not until eleven. I have a class," I said.

"Naked?" Horace said.

"Just the face," Monica said.

I could tell Stephanie was trying to figure out my relationship with Monica. She wanted to be part of the gang, which meant getting along with everybody. She suspected I liked Monica, so I tried not to give more of myself away.

"Can I see your paintings sometime, Monica?" Stephanie said.

"Sure, anytime," Monica said.

I left for class, thinking that I had already got myself in trouble. I didn't even know how I felt about Stephanie. I had just jumped in feet first. I was positive I had killed any opportunity to be with Monica. I wasn't comfortable leaving Stephanie with Horace; I didn't trust him to keep my private life confidential. As usual, I couldn't concentrate in class. I kept thinking about Stephanie's pussy, and how I wanted to eat her out again.

After my classes, I went up to Monica's studio to pose. She was finishing up a landscape that I didn't particularly care for.

"Sit right here," she said.

"Do I get paid for this?" I said.

"I let you talk to me. That's payment enough," she said.

She began sketching on the canvas, slowly, measuring carefully each line, each curve. After about twenty minutes, she was finished.

"You're done. You can get up now," she said.

I walked around to look at the sketch and was pleasantly surprised. It wasn't perfect, but she had caught my likeness, particularly my eyes.

"How are you going to paint it without me posing for you?" I said.

"I'm trying something different. I'm going to paint different colors on your face, like a mask, something between a mask and a portrait," she said.

"That sounds great," I said.

"I want it to look androgynous and multi-ethnic or cross cultural," she said.

"Have you tried it before?" I said.

"Here, look at this one," she said, as she reached into a small stack of canvasses. She pulled out a beautiful painting of a face with a sunset behind it. It looked almost like an African piece of work.

"Wow! That's interesting," I said. "Whose face is it?"

"Actually, this is not a portrait. I just invented a face," she said.

I had seen many masks before. I could not help but think of Picasso, but this face was unique. It could have been a portrait of somebody, either a man or a woman, but it had a symbolic quality that made me think.

"Have you done any other faces like this?" I said.

"Only a few. This is a new adventure for me," she said.

"If you were to add a body to the face and complete the figure, how would you do the body?"

"That's funny. That's exactly what I've been thinking about, and I'm not sure what to do with the bodies," she said.

"Perhaps you should continue the pattern of the face all the way down so that the figure is between nude and clothed," I said.

"That's a good idea," she said.

Horace came up to take a look. Then we left school to take our usual trip downtown. I told him about Monica's ideas as we walked through the cobblestone streets, and he listened carefully, until finally, he stopped me.

"You know, usually my philosophy is to fuck every girl available, but this time it's different; you fucked up," he said.

"What do you mean?" I said.

"It's obvious you're in love with Monica, but now she'll never touch you," he said.

"Thanks for explaining that to me, as if I didn't know," I said.

Suddenly a wave of sadness overcame me, and I imagined Monica and I in a loft in New York, painting and writing, and having all kinds of interesting friends. Then I imagined us living in a villa on a hilltop outside of Florence with Renaissance art all over the house and little bambinos rattling off Italian. I didn't know at that time that Monica would end up doing graduate work at Syracuse University, and that our friendship would continue.

When Horace and I arrived at the apartment, we found John playing cards with a new student named George. He would become one of our good friends and was a painter himself.

"Hey, what's up?" I said.

"Guys, this is George," John said.

"I'm Horace. This is Paul."

"Nice to meet you," George said.

"You're staying for dinner," I said to George.

"Okay, twist my arm," he said.

George was cool, definitely a ladies' man. You could tell by his looks and disposition. His hair was thick, black, and curly, and he had soft features with piercing black eyes. He was very relaxed, and his smile was gentle. George laughed softly and easily. He was instantly likeable.

"Where are you from?" I asked.

"Manhattan," he said.

"I'm jealous," I said.

"What about you?" George said.

"I hate to admit it, but I went to high school in Watertown, New York; now I'm in Syracuse," I said.

"Now you're in Florence," he said.

"Good point. Thanks for reminding me," I said.

Horace and I joined the card game; we opened a bottle of wine, and soon we were laughing our asses off.

"I heard you fucked Stephanie," George said.

"It's just a rumor," I said.

"I like Jennifer," George said.

"So do I," I said.

"You can't have them all," he said.

"He's trying though," Horace said, "but he can't get the one he really wants."

"Who's that?" George said.

"Monica," Horace said.

"She's nice," George said. "What about you, John. Who do you like?"

"It's a secret," John said.

George was a welcome addition to our circle. He fit in perfectly. His humor dripped with satiric irony, a typical New Yorker, and his timing was excellent.

"It must be tough being married in a situation like this," George said to Horace.

"There are advantages and disadvantages; Melanie's parents are paying for the trip, so I guess I can't complain," Horace said.

"Being married doesn't stop him from doing whatever the hell he wants," I said, winking at Horace.

Horace poured George and John another glass of wine; a few minutes later, Jesse walked in.

"The women will be here in a couple of hours," Jesse said, as he joined the game.

"Do the girls come over here every night?" George said.

"Pretty much," John said.

"Which ones?" George said.

"Melanie, Monica, Stephanie, Patricia, and whomever else," Jesse said.

"Do you have a dinner party every night?" George said.

"Almost," I said.

"Why don't you invite Jennifer?" Horace said to George.

"Next time I will," he said.

It wasn't long before the wine kicked in, and Horace took over. He loved to turn the conversation toward the raunchy side, just to get us in the proper mood before the women arrived. George didn't even blink when some of the more disgusting images were presented, and he didn't hesitate to pick up the ball and run with it.

"Stephanie's coming back; you must have given her a good fucking," Horace said.

"I was drunk. I couldn't come for a long time, so I think she was fairly satisfied," I laughed.

"Did you squirt it in her mouth?" Horace said.

"Yeah, I didn't fuck her. She wanted to suck on it. I taught her how to do it. She doesn't have much experience," I said.

"So few women can suck a cock properly. They should give a course devoted solely to cock sucking in high school," George said.

"I bet Monica can suck a mean cock," Horace said.

"She doesn't have to have any skill at all. I would come from simply looking at her beautiful face sucking me off," I said.

"You want to become a writer. Why don't you do the world a real favor and write a book about how to suck cock," Horace said.

"What they really need is on the job training," I said.

"My girlfriend's good at it," Jesse said.

"Oh my God, he speaks!" Horace said. "There's hope for you, buddy."

I was starting to get really horny and was looking forward to Stephanie showing up. I decided to slow down on the wine. I didn't want to be drunk when the women got there. I noticed George didn't drink very much, and he wasn't going to be pushed by Horace either.

"We've got to start cooking pretty soon," I said.

"There's plenty of time," Horace said.

A little later, the women arrived, and we were pleasantly surprised to see Jennifer walk in. She had her blonde hair pulled back in a ponytail and was wearing tight jeans like the others. I winked at Melanie. I knew it had been her idea to invite Jennifer, and I noticed George perked right up. Jennifer was shy at first. She hardly said a word and sipped slowly on her glass of wine. Stephanie sat right next to me; apparently she was claiming her territory, which left me little opportunity to flirt with Jennifer. Monica had an amused smile on her face. She was enjoying the politics of the situation. It had been a few days since we hand seen Patricia. I was wondering if John had broken up with her. I would make a point of asking him later on, but he was tight lipped; I would have to pry it out of him.

"How did you get mixed up with this crew, Jennifer?" Horace said. "You seem like a proper woman."

"Appearances are deceiving," Jennifer said.

"Oh, she's going to fit right in," Horace said, as he introduced everybody. "I'll start cooking. You can help me, George."

"I can't cook to save my life," George said.

"You don't have to do much, except keep me company," Horace said.

The kitchen was right next to the dining room, so Horace and George were able to participate in the conversation as they were cooking.

"We always play strip poker, Jennifer. I hope you know how to play!" Horace said.

"I'll sit out the first few hands to get the feel of it," she laughed.

I liked her wit. She was pretty clever, and she was gorgeous, a deadly combination. I could feel Stephanie crowding me, and I didn't like it. I noticed Jennifer would glance away every time I looked her right in the eyes; I thought it might mean she liked me but was shy. There was going to be competition with George, which didn't bother me much. I enjoyed the sport.

"I would like to play," Stephanie said.

"Not me," Monica said.

"Not tonight," Horace said. "We've got a couple of rookies. We'll have to break them in first."

Stephanie put her hand on my thigh, and I pushed it away immediately. The pasta was ready, with a new sauce invented by Horace. He hated to repeat himself in the kitchen. Everybody ate heartily, but the conversation kept going.

"Do you have a boyfriend in the States, Jennifer?" Horace said.

"Sort of," she said.

"We'll take care of that," he said.

"What school do you go to?" I said.

"Smith," she said.

"My mother and grandmother went there," I said.

"What about you?" she said.

"Syracuse," I said.

"I went to the school of hard knocks; that's why I know so much more than you punks," Horace said.

I noticed George was laying back, not showing much interest, playing it cool.

After the pasta, Horace served breaded veal cutlets and spinach. I knew he was trying to make a good impression for our new guests. He wasn't as vocal as usual. I wanted to talk to Jennifer one on one, but it was impossible; I would have to wait for another opportunity.

"What's your field of study?" George asked Jennifer.

"Art history, but I'm not sure what period I'm going to

concentrate on," she said.

"I'm a painter," he said.

George was making his move. He knew there was nothing more interesting to an art history major than a painter. After dinner the wine flowed freely, the conversation got loud, and there were always two or three people talking at the same time. I noticed Stephanie was particularly quiet, and Jennifer was the center of attention, though she wasn't seeking it.

"Let's go into the bedroom," Stephanie said.

"Later," I said.

She frowned and started to pout, which irritated me. I realized at that moment that Stephanie and I were not going to be able to stay together. She was too possessive, and I was fascinated with Jennifer. Of course Horace noticed all of this as he told me later, and had surmised as much even before I had. Monica was the most perceptive of all. It was as if she could read minds, know what a person was going to say before they said it.

"What's this boyfriend of yours like, Jennifer?" George asked.

"He's fairly tall, good looking, and pretty smart," she said.

"What's he studying?" George asked.

"History and political science; he wants to go to law school," she said.

"Not another lawyer!" Horace said.

"He's a good guy," Jennifer said, "but I'm not madly in love or anything."

"You need to be with an artist," Monica said. "Only the artist can keep a woman interested her whole life," she added, winking at George.

"I think I'd rather be alone," Jennifer said. "I don't need a man to fulfill me. I want to have a career and the freedom to travel whenever I want to."

"You'll change your mind when you get a little older," Horace said.

The fact that Jennifer didn't want a man didn't surprise me. A lot of the young women felt that way; they were not brought up to think of getting married young and settling down. I noticed Monica was drinking more than usual, and was quite talkative; I wondered if she had a crush on George.

"Come on, Horace, you're slipping. My wine glass is empty!" Monica said.

"Excuse me. Coming right up," Horace said, laughing.

Monica had a sparkle in her eye. She kept looking over at George and even winked at him a few times. He was having a great time, and I was a little jealous. The more I concentrated on Jennifer, the more Stephanie bugged me to leave the group.

"Let's go into the bedroom. I want to suck your cock," Stephanie whispered in my ear.

I gave her an irritated look, and suddenly she got up and stomped out of the room. Everyone stopped talking and looked at me.

I got up immediately and followed Stephanie into the bedroom.

"What's wrong with you?" I said.

"You're not paying any attention to me; I know you like Monica and Jennifer more than me!" she said.

"Nonsense. It's a party. I can't just talk to you!" I said.

"You want to fuck Jennifer. Admit it!" she screamed.

"Keep your voice down. Do you think you own me or something, just because we screwed a couple of times?" I said.

"You're a fucking asshole!" she said.

I sat on the bed next to her and calmed down. She started crying, which always made me feel horrible. I very rarely felt like crying, and seeing someone else feeling that way saddened me. I kissed her on the neck and ear.

"Don't cry, sweetheart. I'm sorry," I said.

"I'm falling in love with you, Paul. You don't understand," she said. "I don't just fuck men for the fun of it."

I didn't say anything, because I was thinking that I wasn't in love with her and did fuck her for the fun of it.

"You're just infatuated," I said.

"I know how I feel," she said.

I kissed her again on the neck behind the ear and slipped my tongue inside her ear. She turned to me and opened her mouth, letting me kiss her passionately. It didn't take long before I had an erection.

"I'm so wet," she said.

I unbuttoned her jeans and slid my hand under her panties. She was dripping, and her long clitoris was very sensitive. She pulled her pants off, and I dove into her pussy with my tongue penetrating her lips. I rolled her clitoris between my lips and tongue, driving her wild.

"Are you falling in love with me?" she said.

"Yes," I said.

I thrust my tongue deep into her cunt and grabbed her tight little ass.

"I want your cock inside me," she moaned.

"I want you to lick my anus," I said, surprising myself, because I had never asked such a thing before.

"I will," she said.

I rolled over and spread my legs. She rubbed her tits on my ass and then licked my ass, finally arriving at the deep, dark hole. It felt so good to have my anus licked. After a couple of minutes, I reached orgasm and turned quickly around to come in her mouth. She sucked my cock greedily, getting every drop.

"I never did that before," she said.

"I never had that done to me," I said.

"How did it feel?" she said.

"That was one of the most pleasurable sensations I've ever had," I said.

"Good," she said.

She wanted to talk some more, but all I wanted to do was fall asleep. I could tell she was angry, but I just rolled over and passed out.

Chapter Twenty-Eight

I woke up early as usual and was grateful that I didn't have a hangover. Stephanie was sound asleep, so I slipped out of bed without waking her. John was already up drinking his cappuccino. We decided to go for a run, but it was very cold out, so we put on a few layers. Nothing is more beautiful than Florence early in the morning. The spires of the churches rise peacefully toward the skies, and the birds are busy singing, planning their day. John and I were getting in pretty good shape; I timed our run, noticing that we had shaved off a couple of minutes.

"Did Stephanie calm down last night?" John said, as we were running.

"Yeah. She was all right after she had me all to herself," I said.

"That's probably not going to last, is it?" he said.

"No, I don't think so. She's too possessive," I said.

Now I had to think about dumping Stephanie, and I wasn't thrilled about it. I could imagine her making a scene and dragging my already feeble reputation further down. When we got back to the apartment, Stephanie was in the shower, and I wasn't looking forward to walking to school with her. John took off, and I noticed Jesse had already left. I made cappuccino for Stephanie, and I waited impatiently for her to finish showering.

"I feel great," she said, as she walked by me with a towel on. She noticed I wasn't as cheerful.

"Grumpy this morning?" she said.

"A little, I guess," I said.

I was very quiet on the way to school, and when we passed by the David, I thought he looked like a guy pretending to be tough and heroic, but really full of insecurity. Stephanie tried to cheer me up, but the more she talked, the more irritated I got. I was relieved to arrive at school, where I could sit with Horace and laugh a little. I wanted to know what Jennifer and Monica had said after Stephanie and I had gone into the bedroom. Horace had his classic evil smile plastered on his face when I walked into the café.

"How was it?" he said.

"What?" I said.

"The angry sex," he said.

"Pretty good," I laughed. "What did the girls think about it all?" I said.

"They got a big kick out of it. Jennifer said: 'Paul's quite the stud.

"I can't believe what a jerk I am," I said. "Now my chances with Jennifer are about zero."

"Not necessarily," he said. "These girls love the competition. Why do you think you're doing so well? If the odds weren't so dramatically in your favor, you'd be struggling like the rest of us." He laughed.

"I have to break up with Stephanie now. She's really getting on my nerves," I said.

"Do it right away. It's not going to be pleasant. The sooner you get it over with, the better," he said.

"Do you think Monica's interested in George?" I said.

"Where did that come from?" he said.

"I don't know. The way she was looking at him and flirting

with him, I think she has a crush on him," I said.

Horace burst out laughing.

"She's fucking with you," he said. "She's playing one against the other. I'm sure she likes him, but he's not going to get anywhere with her either," he said.

"How do you know? What are you a mind reader?" I said.

"You've got a lot to learn." He laughed.

Jennifer came into the café, and Horace motioned her to sit with us. She looked great. Her blonde hair was pulled back, and she was only wearing a hint of makeup. She had jeans on with a sweatshirt, looking very athletic.

"Have fun last night, Paul?" she said.

"Not really," I said.

"Stephanie is a little temperamental," she said.

"Yeah," I said, hoping someone would change the conversation.

"George is a nice guy," she said.

"He's great," Horace said, "a perfect addition to our group."

"Have you guys ever seen his work?" she asked.

"No," we said in unison.

"Maybe he needs a model," Horace said, winking at her.

"I charge a lot of money. I don't think he can afford me," she said.

I was jealous listening to her talk about George. I could see she was already trying to steer clear of me. I decided I was going to break up with Stephanie that day; I wasn't going to wait. After classes, I asked Stephanie if she wanted to walk down to the market with me. She agreed, but I'm sure she didn't notice I was upset. We talked about all kinds of things while I tried to find the right words to let her down easy.

"I don't know how to put this; I don't want to hurt your feelings, but our relationship is not working out," I said softly.

"I knew this was coming," she said. "You're not really giving it much of a chance, are you?"

"Listen, Steph, I'm sorry if you feel I took advantage of you, but we're here for only a few months. I can't be tied down while I'm in Italy. Last night you wouldn't even let me be with my friends," I said.

The hard part was over with. Now I first had to stick to my guns without backing down.

"I was a little drunk last night. I wasn't in control of my emotions. I'll give you more space. I promise," she said.

"I can't really, Steph. Maybe we shouldn't have jumped into bed so quickly. That was my mistake, but I'm not in love with you. I'm sorry," I said.

"Well, I'm not in love with you either!" she said, turning around and walking in the other direction.

I felt relieved. It was over with, and I was proud of myself for getting right to the point. I went to the market and bought fresh meat and vegetables, taking my time and talking to my favorite vendors. It was cold out, but the walk had warmed me up, and I felt good. I was hoping John or Jesse would be home so that I could talk about my crazy love life. Not that they were interested, but I just needed to let off some steam. Fortunately, John was home.

"What did you buy? I'm starving," he said.

"I got some chicken, and our favorite soft cheese," I said.

"How about bread?" he said.

"Of course," I said.

"Are you going to cook? I just want some of that bread and cheese," he said.

"I don't think I'm going to cook," I said. "I broke up with Stephanie," I blurted out.

"Good," he said. "How did she take it?"

"Pretty well, really. She didn't scream or call me names, or hit me." I laughed.

"She's a good kid; now you'll have to see what she says about you to the other women," he said.

"I'm sure she'll trash me," I said.

"Probably," he said.

I thought about Stephanie telling Jennifer and Monica all kinds of terrible things about me, not to mention what she might say to the other women whom I had not gotten to know yet. John and I feasted on bread and cheese.

Then I took a nice nap. I had an awful dream though. My mind was still dealing with the echo of my breaking up with Stephanie. In the dream, I was making love to Jennifer, Stephanie, and Monica at the same time, a ménage a quattro, reaching peaks of ecstasy never reached before. I was fucking Monica up the ass, while Stephanie and Jennifer were eating each other out. Then, of course, we rotated until everyone had sucked and fucked each other. Then, suddenly, things took a turn for the worst. As I was coming in Monica's mouth, she bit down hard on my cock, making me scream.

"Why did you bite me?" I yelled.

"Because you fucked Jennifer before you fucked me!" Monica said.

She hadn't drawn blood, but I was in terrible pain. Jennifer said she would make me feel better and began sucking on my cock slowly, eventually making me hard again. Just as I was about to squirt it in her mouth, she bit me too. I screamed again, and the girls all laughed.

"Why? Why?" I said.

"Because we love you!" they said in unison.

Then Stephanie started on me, sucking me ever so slowly, every so tenderly, making me harder than a rock. I was scared that she was going to bite me, but just as I was about to come, she squeezed the top of my cock and destroyed the sensation. At that point, I woke up.

"Jesus," I said.

I took a shower, laughing at my dream, but I wondered if it had some deep meaning. John and I played cards for a while, but I couldn't get any information out of him about his relationship. He was tight lipped, and I wished I could keep some things to myself. A little later, Jesse showed up with Horace, who had brought more food. They sat down to play cards with us, and I wondered what women were going to show up for dinner, if any.

"I broke up with Steph," I said to Horace.

"How'd it go?"

"Okay, I guess, but I wish I had handled myself differently at the beginning," I said.

"You'll learn," he said. "So who's next on the list? Jennifer?"

"I think I'm going to cool it for awhile; I've got to get off this emotional roller coaster," I said.

We played for several hours until the women showed up. I was glad Jennifer returned, along with Monica and Melanie. I wondered if George was going to come over, and then it occurred to me that maybe the girls had come to see him. Jennifer was wearing really tight jeans. I couldn't take my eyes off her crotch, and I'm sure she noticed. Monica had her hair in pigtails and looked cute as hell. I could tell it was going to be a very frustrating evening, just fantasizing about these two, without much chance of success. George did show up a little later, and Horace started to loosen up with a couple of glasses of wine. I could tell it was going to be an interesting night, so I began pouring wine for the women, hoping that somehow I could get something started with Jennifer. So much for getting off the roller coaster!

"I heard you broke up with Stephanie," Monica said.

"Word travels fast," I said.

"She wasn't your type," George said.

"What is my type?" I said.

"You need a strong, independent woman; one who will bring you to your knees and make you beg for her attention!" he said.

I burst out laughing, and so did the others, but I was thinking he was absolutely right.

"What's your type?" Monica said to George.

"The same." George laughed.

It occurred to me that it was an issue of dominance. Maybe I was a dominant person over most women, but really wanted to be dominated by a woman. If there was no challenge, if the woman simply submitted, I quickly lost interest. Monica could make me submit; I would be her slave, do anything she said, follow her around like a little puppy. But right now she seemed more interested in George, and I was definitely jealous. I decided to concentrate on Jennifer. Maybe she could dominate me too.

Horace started cooking. He said he had learned a new recipe and that we were in for a real treat. I was sitting next to Jennifer and across from Monica, while George was on my other side. Jen was wearing a loose, low-cut blouse, and it didn't take me long to realize she wasn't wearing a bra. I didn't want to be too obvious, but every time she leaned over to pick up her glass of wine, I got a good look at her nipples. She had beautiful, small breasts. They looked firm and tasty.

"George, why are you so secretive about your paintings? I noticed your studio was locked and nobody has seen any of your work," Monica said.

"I'm doing some experiments right now. I don't want anybody to see them or make any comments," he said.

"What kind of experiments?" Jennifer said.

"With space mostly. I'm working on an illusion between inside and outside, altering what might be perceived as a 'normal' space," he said.

"Sounds interesting," Jen said.

Jen leaned over again to pick up her glass, and just as I was getting a good look at her breasts, she looked over and caught me peeking. She smiled and leaned back casually. Then, to my great surprise, she leaned over again, a few minutes later, giving me a good, long look. I almost burst out laughing, but it was then that I realized Jennifer was interested in me.

"Are you using color also to make the illusion work?" Monica asked.

"I'm trying," he said.

"I want to see them," she said.

"I'll show you mine, if you show me yours!" she laughed.

"Maybe we can work something out," he said, winking.

"How's it coming?" I said to Horace.

"This is going to take a little longer than usual," he said. "This is not just your average dish. Hey, can I have a little more wine, please?" he added.

I poured wine for everybody, thinking that I would keep

filling Jennifer's glass to see what might happen. After a few more glasses, Jennifer kept leaning over, giving me a great view. I noticed she was getting a little louder and more boisterous, so at one point I decided to rub my leg against hers. I took my shoe off and slipped my toes up her tight jeans. She pretended not to notice, and a minute later, rubbed her foot against my leg.

"Time to eat!" Horace yelled. We all got up and grabbed a dish, helping ourselves to yet another chicken masterpiece. Horace always cooked for an army. There was plenty to go around. Jennifer ate very lightly, while Monica, even though she was very trim, ate heartily.

"I feel so untalented around all of you. Do you paint too, Paul?" Jennifer said.

"No, I would like to be a writer," I said.

"What have you written so far?" she asked.

"One long short story," I said.

"It takes a few years," George said.

"I'm determined to write a novel after I graduate," I said.

"You'll do it." Jennifer smiled.

The food was so good; we hardly said a word for the next fifteen minutes. Jennifer and I were playing footsie throughout dinner, and she was making me really horny. We decided to go out for ice cream afterwards. We all loved to walk through the cobblestone streets in the evening. It was a cold February night, and the streets were wet from the rain. The city glistened with lights. The dark church spires loomed over buildings and streets giving a mystical aura. Sometimes, walking in Florence made me feel like it was still the fifteenth century, with statues protruding from buildings, and the architecture unchanged for many centuries.

Jennifer and I fell behind the others a few yards, so that we could talk privately.

"I'm glad you've become part of our gang," I said.

"You guys are a lot of fun," she said.

"Too bad you didn't come in September, but maybe you can stay through the summer?" I said.

"Can you believe that girl Audrey already went back home because she couldn't stand it here?" she said.

"She'll be even more miserable at home. It doesn't matter where people go; they either thrive or die," I said.

"I want to live in New York City one day," she said.

"I do too," I said.

I held her hand as we walked, and I felt like I was in love. As usual, I imagined us married, living in a penthouse suite in New York, this time with just one child, in the middle of the art world. She had delicate hands, which were stronger than they seemed, because she was a great tennis player, the best on her college team. I teased her and made her laugh. She was sharp; for every wise remark I made at her, she had a similarly wise retort.

"We should play some tennis in the spring," I said.

"How good are you?" she said.

"I was number one in high school, but I don't play very much now. I can beat the pants off of you though," I said.

"We'll see," she said, "but I'm not going to sport you any points."

"You know what I'd really like to do?" I said.

"What?" she said.

"I'd like to take you to Venice for a weekend," I said.

"We could do that," she said.

"When should we go?" I said.

"How about two weeks?" she said.

"Great," I said.

I was elated, not only did I have a new girlfriend, but we were going to the most romantic city in the world. I started fantasizing about pulling off her tight jeans and diving into her muff. I couldn't help myself. At that age, lust and love were irrevocably linked. She had the cutest little ass. All I wanted to do was kiss her and squeeze that little ass. It was great eating ice cream late at night in the middle of the city.

There were several people eating outside the shop. We hung around talking until it was time to go home. Everybody went in different directions, and I gave Jen a kiss goodnight.

Chapter Twenty-Nine

I slept very well, and woke up feeling great. John and I went running, and he kept teasing me about Jennifer.

"She knows your MO There's no way she's going to fuck you," he laughed.

"Horace says they love the competition," I said.

"She's going to make you jump through hoops; you're going to be on your knees, telling her you love her, and she still won't give it up," he said.

It was a crisp, clear morning. Traffic was just beginning to move. We ran out toward the fort, up the hill, and could see the entire city. The landscape was so breathtaking, it made us run harder. We were getting into better shape. We were running under seven minute miles and climbed the hills with little difficulty.

"We're going to Venice in a couple of weeks," I said.

"She's going to Venice with you?" he said.

"Yeah. Tell me she's not going to fuck me in Venice," I said.

"She might," he said.

When we got to the fort, we took a break and just stood in awe of the city. It occurred to me that the beauty of the city was the product, and the cause, of the great art within it. One had to feel optimistic, in love, and beautiful to produce great art. That wasn't right either. There was a great deal of beautiful, often tragic art that was produced under horrible conditions.

We ran quickly and freely down the hill, back to the apartment. We cooled off for half an hour and took quick showers, realizing we were late for school. I wasn't surprised to see Horace talking to Jennifer in the café. He was an instigator and loved to be in the middle of the action.

"Hey you," he yelled at me, "we're talking about you."

"Keep it down to a dull roar," I said, "I hope you're not telling her anything too personal."

"Just about your other love affairs." He laughed.

"Oh great. Don't listen to anything he says, Jen. He lies!" I said.

"I'm finding his stories very interesting. You're quite a character," she said.

"He exaggerates," I said.

We sat for a while, talking about various things; I noticed she was getting comfortable around us, loosening up a bit, talking freely, and laughing a lot. George joined us a little later. He leaned back in his chair and smoked a small cigar, as if he owned the world.

"What's for dinner?" George asked Horace.

"I don't know. We'll scrape up something," he said. "Coming over?"

I'd love to," George said.

"Bring Monica with you," Horace said.

"You're coming, aren't you?" I said to Jennifer.

"Be glad to," she said.

Even though I was starting to date Jennifer, I was jealous of George and Monica, but Monica was still aloof. She wasn't taking any bait. George pulled out a small sketchbook and began doing a portrait of Jennifer with little dots, his version of pointillism. In five minutes, he was done, and it was one of the most amazing little sketches I had ever seen. This guy had talent. Jennifer laughed with excitement.

"Can I keep it?" she said.

"Of course," George said.

"Do one of me," Horace said.

"Tomorrow," George said.

I wanted to see George's paintings. I thought maybe we had a genius on our hands. I wished I could paint, but it would be several years before I learned how to paint. I didn't think I had any talent in that direction, but as I found out years later, my father's father had been a very talented painter in Rome. My father recounted this to me as I woke up in the morning as a boy, surrounded by his father's great reproductions of the Impressionists.

After class, George, Horace, and I walked downtown to shop for food. All we talked about was women and drugs.

"Have you ever been in a threesome?" George asked Horace.

"When there's cocaine around, threesomes are very common," he said with a grin.

"Did you ever do cocaine?" I asked George.

"A couple of times," he said. "It's total shit," he added.

"I quit that," Horace said.

"My freshman year at Hobart, I smoked quite a lot of pot, but I stopped after spending the summer with my father," I said.

"Does Melanie get into anything?" George asked Horace.

"Doesn't touch a thing," he said. "I don't like a woman who has to be fucked up to fuck."

The streets were busy. Every Italian walks around drinking espresso. They're thin and they move and talk quickly. There were cars trying to squeeze through the narrow streets. They never hesitated to use their horns. The sidewalks were usually wide enough for only one person, so we either walked in single file on the walk or spilled out into the streets. Scooters screamed by with youngsters in them. If you didn't pay attention, you might get hit by one of them. All this noise and confusion added to the vitality of the city.

"Does Melanie say anything about your drug use and drinking?" I said to Horace.

"Not a word," he said. "She gets tipsy after a glass or two of wine and doesn't pay any attention to me."

George wanted to know about Monica. We told him what we knew, but added that she was quite the mysterious woman. He knew I was interested in her too, but there was no woman in the world who would keep us from being friends.

"Jennifer seems to be a proper woman. Is she wild enough for you?" George asked me.

"I don't know. With my track record, this probably won't last very long, but I think she's incredibly sexy. Maybe she'll have some power over me," I said.

We arrived at the market, which was teeming with people. We watched Horace in amazement as he dealt with the vendors in his very broken Italian. We pooled our money and bought all kinds of food. When we got to the apartment, we played cards as usual, and waited for the others to show up. Jennifer showed up early. I brought her into my room to show her all the pictures I had taken of Europe. We sat on the bed very close to each other, flirting and talking softly to each other.

"I want to kiss you," I said.

"You may." She smiled.

I put my arms around her and kissed her on each eye,

before I moved down to her mouth. She had the most sensuous lips. As we embraced and began kissing passionately, Horace pounded on the door.

"Hey, you two, cut it out. It's time to be social, not to hide in your room," he said loudly.

"We are being social," I said. "Let's go out there. We can resume this later."

"You're just jealous," Jennifer said to Horace.

"I know you want me," he said.

A little later Monica and Melanie showed up. They were laughing hysterically, and we couldn't figure out why.

"We're talking about you guys," Melanie said. "We were imagining Horace posing in his briefs for a painting."

"Hey, I look good naked or in briefs," he said in mock seriousness.

"I also asked Melanie if his moustache tickled," Monica said.

"Jennifer, has Paul showed you his pictures yet?" Melanie said.

"As a matter of fact…" Jen laughed.

We played cards for a while, but instead of cooking, John talked us into going out for dinner. Our favorite trattoria was down the street a little ways. It was early; we had no trouble putting two tables together. Horace ordered the wine. When we went out, we always had Chianti, either a '71 or '73; all the odd years of the seventies were good. Jennifer and I were sitting so close together, I could smell her perfume. I wanted to take her home and fuck her right then.

"I'm leaving Melanie and marrying Monica," Horace said, as he opened the first bottle.

"Well, at least you won't have to change the monogrammed

towels," John said.

"You've pulled that trick too many times," Melanie said.

I spread my legs, pushing my knee against Jennifer's, and imagined us on a gondola in Venice, kissing and holding each other as we passed through the canals.

"Maybe we should rent a big, beautiful villa on the outskirts of Florence and all live there in sin and debauchery like a Fellini film," Horace said.

"We'd get kicked out of Italy," John said.

I put my hand on Jen's thigh, but she promptly removed it.

She gave me a look that said: "Not now, later!"

We all ordered pasta since we were on limited budgets, and ordered more and more bread before the pasta came out. The wine was fantastic, a dry, rich, full-bodied flavor that stayed with you. George was sitting next to Monica. Often, during dinner, the two of them talked quietly to each other as though they were alone.

"Have you been to Venice this year?" Jen asked me.

"No. I haven't been there since I was a kid," I said.

"I can't wait to go," she said.

"I want to make love to you," I whispered in her ear.

"Down boy," she said.

It didn't take long for the food to come out. The pasta was homemade. It was out of this world. We ate voraciously and hardly talked through the meal. I kept watching Monica, trying to read her expressions. She seemed fascinated with George.

I compared Jennifer to Monica, listing qualities, trying to weight them like so many ounces of gold. Jen was quick, had a masterful wit that penetrated deeply, teamed with a warm smile and a spark in her eye. Monica was more sensuous. She didn't have to say anything; she was a queen, and she knew it. The queen bee enjoys her status, watching all the worker bees cater to her every whim.

And George was a king, not influenced by other people. The city had made him worldlier than the subtlest diplomat. He moved through space like a cat, able to pounce at any moment, but preferring to observe the folly of others. After dinner, we walked through the dark, narrow streets. The city was quiet, and there was a chill in the air. I held Jen's hand; her skin was so soft and her touch so gentle.

Back at the apartment, the others played cards, while Jennifer and I went into my bedroom. I kissed her as soon as we sat on the bed, but she kept pushing my groping hands away. She wanted to talk, and I wanted to make love.

"Why don't you tell me about Venice?" she said.

"Everybody who goes there makes love and never sees the city," I said.

"Well, we're going to see everything," she said.

"I hope so," I said.

Finally, she gave in. Her tongue flitted around my mouth; she put one leg over mine, opening herself up. I put my hand between her legs, massaging her pussy. She groaned in ecstasy. I slid two fingers inside her; she was incredibly wet. Then I pulled her jeans off and her panties, which was always the most exciting part of foreplay. I stood up while she sat on the bed; she unbuttoned my pants and slid them down far enough for my erect cock to jump out. I grabbed my cock and gently slapped it against her face, making her giggle.

"My, it's so big!" she teased.

"The better to serve you with," I said.

I pushed her down on the bed and wrapped my arms around

her ass, sticking my tongue in her cunt. There was no taste, just a slippery feeling and fresh scent. I climbed up on her and tried to insert my cock, but she was too tight. I spread her legs further and pushed her knees up to her head. This time I got in, and she let out a great moan. She was so tight, it was unbelievable; I felt like she was actually gripping my cock.

She wanted to kiss, while we made love. I was used to burying my face in the pillow and concentrating, but she opened her mouth and devoured my tongue. She felt so aroused, she said:

"I love you; I love fucking you."

After a few minutes, I could feel myself coming, so I pulled out and came all over her belly. She hadn't orgasmed, and I asked her about it.

"I can come sometimes, but it takes a lot of effort," she said.

I began licking her again, and inserted two fingers, rubbing her g-spot. Slowly but surely she got closer and closer to orgasm. I licked her for what seemed an eternity, and finally she came. Juices actually squirted out of her pussy, and she let out a small scream. I was sure the others had heard her. She pulled me up to her and said:

"Thank you. That was great."

We were too exhausted to put on our clothes and join the party, so we went to sleep, our bodies pressed together like spoons.

Chapter Thirty

The next morning, we awoke refreshed; we had made love again in the middle of the night and had slept well. Jen wanted to go home first to change before going to school, but we stopped at a café to get our coffee. On the way, we passed the statue of David; he looked like a proud stud that morning, completely possessed of his manhood.

Jennifer and I were very cheerful. We got along perfectly. All of our thoughts blended well together. The two of us talked about Venice, and I told her about Sicily. We wanted to travel everywhere. I thought I was in love, and I know she felt the same way. She decided not to go home first after all.

Horace had a big grin on his face when we arrived at school.

"There are the love birds," he said.

George was sitting with him and made room for us to sit down.

"You have a big smile on your face this morning, Jennifer." Horace laughed.

"Nothing like Italy to lift your spirits," Jennifer said. "I suppose everybody knows already, right, Horace? You couldn't keep your mouth shut," she added.

"I haven't said anything," he said.

Jennifer just smiled and shook her head.

"You think anybody will notice you're wearing the same clothes as yesterday?" Horace said.

"I don't care," Jen said.

After classes, Horace, George, and I went to the market downtown. I told the boys some of the details of my lovemaking. They cracked up when I told them she was sucking me off and I squirted my come right in her eyes, which wasn't true. I really liked Jennifer, but that didn't prevent me from talking about her in a raunchy way. We bought a lot of food, always three or four kinds of cheeses and plenty of wine.

As usual, we played cards and entertained that night.

Jennifer and Monica seemed to be becoming close friends. We didn't see Ellen very much any more, and there was a rumor going around that Monica had a boyfriend. The boyfriend was supposedly Italian. It wasn't George; we knew that. But Monica was tight lipped about it.

Jennifer spent the nights with me for the next couple of weeks. Our lovemaking was intense. She was a good lover and tried hard to please me. I wanted to fuck her up the ass, but she would have no part of it. Finally, it was time to go to Venice. We were looking so forward to it. It was March. There wouldn't be any tourists. We had to find a cheap room and economize as much as possible.

We found a tiny room with two single beds, which we immediately pushed together. We weren't there five minutes before we were fucking our brains out. Exhausted, we slept for a long time, then showered and dressed for dinner. Jen and I discovered an inexpensive trattoria in a small piazza not far from our pensione. We ordered the house wine and a simple plate of pasta.

"What are you going to do when you return to the States?" she asked me.

"I'm planning to go to law school, but I would like to take some time off to write a novel," I said.

"Will you come see me?" she said.

"Of course," I said.

"What are you going to write about?" she said.

"I don't know yet."

After dinner, we took the most romantic walk ever, along small canals with tiny bridges, the stars and moon shining above.

"I love you," she said at one point, as we were standing on a little bridge, the lights from the houses reflecting on the water.

"I love you too," I said.

We walked with our arms around each other, the real world nowhere to be seen. After a few hours, tired from walking, we returned to the hotel. We drank some wine and ate cheese with bread. It had been a perfect day, and we were looking forward to a long night of lovemaking. After about three glasses of wine, she started getting silly and very horny; I asked her to do a little strip tease for me. We didn't have any music, so we sang a little bit as she danced. For an amateur, she was unbelievable. Jennifer was wearing her tight jeans and a sweater, her body slim and sexy. The sweater came off first as she gyrated her ass. She had small, perky breasts stuffed into a light, silky bra. Jennifer sat on my lap, giggling, her ass sliding up and down on my hard cock, which I had taken out of my pants.

Then her jeans came off; they were so tight, she had to struggle to pull them off. She was wearing white panties that outlined every nuance of her pussy. I wanted to fuck her right then, but she made me wait, teasing my cock with her tongue.

"You're so hard!" she said.

I grabbed her and threw her down on the bed, biting her

panties. I tore them off with my mouth and starting eating her out. She came immediately.

"Fuck me! Fuck me!" she screamed.

Without hesitating, I rolled her over and put a pillow under her crotch, entering her from behind. I grabbed her hair and fucked her as hard as I could. She came again.

"I'm coming!" I said.

She turned around, put my cock in her mouth and I unloaded. I kept squirting and squirting until she had to open her mouth and let it dribble down her chin. She swallowed hard and kept sucking to get every drop.

"Wow!" I said.

"That was fantastic," she said.

Worn out, we fell asleep almost immediately and slept pretty late. We made love again in the morning, but it was not as intense as the night before. Then we showered and went out to look for coffee and something to eat. There was a small café not far from our hotel, where we sat and sipped our cappuccino, listening to the locals.

Jen and I wanted to see several churches. I wanted to study the early movement away from the Renaissance, particularly Tintoretto, who fascinated me. The churches didn't open until a little later, so we walked to Piazza San Marco and just hung out for a while. The two us couldn't walk anywhere without holding hands; we felt so much in love.

I was so infatuated with her at one point I said:

"We should get married."

"I agree," she said, kissing me.

My heart was pounding; I couldn't believe I had said it and was shocked she had consented. We didn't speak for a long time after that; we walked on air, absorbing the atmosphere of the city. Eventually, one of the churches we wanted to see opened up; we took our time seeing every painting, but as soon as we walked out, I realized nothing had really registered. All I could think about was marrying this girl and dragging her back to the hotel to make love to her.

"How many children do you want to have?" she said.

"Two or three," I said.

"Perfect," she said.

"Let's go back to the hotel," I said, squeezing her hand.

As we were walking back, Jennifer got curious about Horace.

"How did you guys become friends? You're so different!" she said.

"All my friends have a sense of humor. Humor cuts across all boundaries; it's the one main trait that binds my friends and me. I can't stand being around people who have no sense of humor. If Horace had grown up in a different family, he might have been more like me. He studies with Melanie and is really smart, but he came from a very poor family; he didn't have the advantages we had," I said.

"I like him. Don't misunderstand me. It's just that you two are so different," she said. "Now George is more like you, very sophisticated, cool."

"You think I'm cool, do you?" I laughed.

"Very cool," she said.

"I'm not trying to be cool," I said.

"That's why you are," she said.

When we got back to the hotel room, we fucked our brains out, and I came in her mouth again, a true sign somebody loves you. We fell asleep holding each other very closely and slept for a long time. Later we went out for cappuccino and talked some more.

"Are you planning to stay in Syracuse, I mean for graduate study?" she said.

"I think so, but I might go to North Carolina for a while to live with Horace and Melanie to write my first novel," I said.

"You're not ready to get married and settle down," she said.

"Maybe not," I said.

That seemed to impact her. She was quiet for a long time, as we thought about our futures. The air was cool; there weren't too many people walking around. The coffee tasted really good. I thought about Monica. I would have married her in a minute. We knew that when we returned to the States, things would be completely different. It would be almost impossible to stay together.

"Do you want to go to that church not too far from here?" I said.

"Sure," she said listlessly.

We held hands again as we walked, but the passion wasn't there. When we entered the church and studied the first painting, we got into an argument about its meaning. It was the first time we had argued, and it felt terrible. Our disagreeable attitudes lasted for the rest of the afternoon. We returned to the hotel in foul moods.

"Let's make peace," I said.

"Truce," she said.

I kissed her, and the next minute we were tearing our clothes off and fucking like rabbits. Our sex was aggressive. I fucked her harder than ever, grunting with every thrust, as if I were trying to hurt her. I fucked her from behind, grabbing her hair and really pulling on it. She loved it. She came again and again. At one point I tried to put it in her ass, but she wouldn't let me. We collapsed after that.

"Nothing like a good argument to stimulate our sex life," she said.

"Let's not make a habit of it," I said.

We went out for dinner, and since it was our last night in Venice, we went to a more expensive restaurant. I ordered a large bottle of wine, and we both got the local catch. By the time we were finished with dinner, we were pretty drunk. We got very sentimental, telling each other we were in love and would stay together no matter now difficult it got. We walked around the streets and canals, holding each other very tightly and kissing all the while. By the time we got back to the hotel, we immediately fell asleep.

In the morning, we woke up with hangovers; we made love tenderly and our headaches went away. Our train left at ten, so we had to hustle to get there on time. We slept most of the way back to Florence.

Chapter Thirty-One

When I got back to the apartment, John wanted to hear the details of my trip, particularly the lovemaking. I exaggerated, of course, and had him in hysterics. I told him that one time she stuck two fingers up my ass while she was blowing me, and how I exploded into her mouth, making her gag.

"Did you fuck her up the ass?" he said.

"I tried but she wouldn't let me," I said, "but I will," I added.

Horace was planning to come over that evening. I knew I would have to tell these stories all over again. As it turned out, John had gotten laid that weekend too, by a girl we didn't know very well. He said he probably wouldn't fuck her again, but we always said that. I took a long nap and later showered for dinner. Horace and George arrived together with bags of food. Sure enough, I had to recount all the details of my trip, including even more details that hadn't happened.

"Are you still in love?" George asked.

"Who the hell knows?" I said.

"Then you're not," Horace said.

"I like being with her, but the subject of marriage came up, and frankly, I'm not ready for that," I said.

"Marriage!" George, Horace, and John said at the same time.

"What do you want from me? I was overcome with passion; I'm telling you she has the tightest pussy in the world!"

I said.

"You wouldn't be the first man who got married for such a stupid reason," Horace said.

"Are you talking about yourself?" I said.

"I've made a few mistakes," he said, winking.

"After you fuck her for a few more weeks, you'll lose the passion," George said. "You've got a lot of women ahead of you."

"I'm tired of going from woman to woman; I just want one," I said.

"And you can't have her," Horace said. "Besides, you're just a kid; you're going to change a lot as you get older. You have no idea what kind of woman you'll want when you're forty," he said.

We started preparing the food and kept talking about women. We opened the wine and toasted to the Italian way of life, wine, women, and song. Horace had us cutting up all kinds of vegetables, but he was keeping his creation a secret. He made a sauce for pasta. I watched him carefully, every step of the way.

"Which women are coming tonight?" I said.

"I think just my wife and Monica," Horace said.

"Good," I said.

"It should be a quiet evening," he said.

He made a white sauce with wine, which I had seen him do before. Then he kicked me out of the kitchen.

"You'd think his cooking was the Manhattan project," I said to George.

"He wouldn't be a real chef without his secrets," George said.

"I forgot; you have your secrets too," I said.

"An interesting man has many," he said. "You must have a few."

"I'm working on it," I said.

A little later, Monica and Melanie showed up. Monica was wearing her tight jeans. I couldn't take my eyes off her ass. They teased me about my trip to Venice, saying that Jennifer must be too tired out to come to dinner.

"What are we eating?" Monica asked.

"It's a secret," I said.

"That's when he's at his best," she said.

We drank for a while, and then sat down to eat. The surprise was duck. It was the most delicious meal I had ever eaten. I sat next to Monica and forgot about Jennifer completely.

"Why don't we go to Venice?" I said to her.

"You just got back," she said.

"So?" I said.

"I don't think Jennifer would be too thrilled about it," she said.

"Just as friends," I said.

"Sure," she said.

"What are you two whispering about?" Horace said.

"Nothing," I said.

The more pressure I put on Monica, the more she resisted. I was so frustrated.

"I hear you have a boyfriend," I said to her.

"Where'd you hear that?"

"The grapevine. Well do you?"

"It's none of your business," she said.

"Is he Italian?"

"Drop it, Paul."

I let it go, and we rejoined the mainstream of conversation. Though I drank more heavily than usual, the food kept me from getting too drunk.

"Do you want to pose for me, Monica?" George said.

"Sure, but not naked," she said.

"No, I just want to do your face," he said.

"What, in some bizarre cubist thing?" she said.

"You'll see," he said.

Following dinner, everyone went home, and I was glad to hit the sack. I slept deeply and woke up late. John and Jesse were already out of the apartment, but I didn't feel like rushing to school. I figured I would miss the first couple of classes and just go to the café and read the paper. I got to school at about ten-thirty, and Horace was the only one sitting in the café, reading a book.

"Hey what's up?" he said.

"Bit of a hangover," I said.

"Jennifer was looking for you," he said.

"I'll catch her when she gets out of class," I said.

"You look depressed," he said.

"No, I'm okay. I just don't feel like my normal self," I said.

"Is Monica mad at you?" he said.

"I hope not. I don't think so," I said.

The cappuccino tasted delicious. After the second cup, I started feeling better. There were only two months left in Florence, and I found myself thinking more and more about the States.

"What are you going to do when you go home?" I said.

"Melanie's got at least another year of school, so we'll be going back to Raleigh, and I'll get a job," he said. "The economy is booming down there. I want to own a restaurant one of these days. What are you going to do?"

"I thought I'd come down south to see you guys and write a novel," I said.

"You're more than welcome."

Jennifer got out of class an hour later; I decided to skip my classes and walk downtown with her. She looked great and was glad to see me. We talked about Venice and our plans for when we returned home. Jennifer wanted to go to graduate school and maybe one day become a journalist.

"When did you come up with this journalist idea?" I said.

"Well, you've been talking so much about writing, I think it would be interesting, but I don't think I could ever write a novel," she said.

"Journalism can be great once you work your way up a little; you can travel to great places and meet interesting people," I said.

The market was busy as usual with people talking very loudly and the vendors hawking their wares. Outdoors were several stands with clothing. Jennifer stopped to look at a suede jacket. I wanted to buy it for her, but I couldn't afford it. The atmosphere of the market was electric, and I felt like I was in love again. We bought some bread, cheese, and meat, and took it to my apartment. John and Jesse were playing cards in the dining room, so Jen and I went into my bedroom. We had a picnic on the floor and looked at photographs from my trip to Sicily.

"Why don't you spend the night?" I said.

"My family won't let me. They have very strict rules," she said.

"You have before," I said.

"I know, but they told me I couldn't do it any more," she said.

"I can't believe it. This country is so backwards in some ways," I said.

"At least it keeps the young girls from getting pregnant," she said.

"True, but you're not a kid," I said.

The cheese was delicious. I ate three or four pieces of bread with it. I wanted to make love, but Jennifer resisted my advances.

"Why do you push me away?" I said.

"I'm not in the mood," she said.

"I think it's more than that," I said.

"You're reading too much into it," she said.

"You think I'm just taking advantage of you," I said.

"No, I don't," she said.

"Yes you do," I said.

"Are you?"

"See, I knew it."

"You sound like a little kid," she said.

I decided to give up and just eat. Suddenly, I was in a bad mood and felt like a spoiled child. I told myself to cut it out and dragged my mind out of the mood.

"We don't have to make love every time we see each other," she said.

"I know. I'm just being a brat," I said.

We took a nap after we ate, and then she went home. I felt frustrated, but decided to hang out with the guys and forget about women for a while.

Chapter Thirty-Two

Our Spring break was coming up. Horace and I wanted to go on a trip to the South again without the women, but he didn't know how Melanie would take it. She complained, but when Monica offered to go to Paris with her, she relented. I was excited; just the two of us on a trip to paradise. We didn't have much money, but enough to take the train to Sicily and back and stay at cheap hotels.

We brought a small bottle of wine with us on the train, which we took early in the morning and were feeling pretty drunk by noon. The Italians in our cabin thought we were strange to be drinking so early in the morning, but we didn't care. We were free, and all we wanted to do was celebrate our freedom. We slept until we got to Messina, and then stood on the side of the ferry after they loaded the train on. The stars were out. It was a splendid night, and excitement was in the air.

"Are you and Jennifer pretty tight still?" he said.

"Yes, I think so; we like each other, but we don't trust each other," I said.

"I can see why she doesn't trust you. But why don't you trust her?" he said.

"I don't know, probably because I can't trust myself," I said.

"Look down there," he said.

Along the side of the ship, not far from us, were two women standing next to the rail, looking out over the water.

They were dressed like Americans but that didn't necessarily mean anything.

"I'll go over first," Horace said.

"What if they don't speak English?" I said.

"Everybody speaks some English," he said.

"You'll fuck it up. Let me go over. If they don't speak English, I'll motion for you," he said.

Horace walked down the ship casually and leaned against the rail next to the closest woman. They were talking for a few minutes, so I figured they spoke English. After a while, he motioned me to come over. I knew we were in.

"This is Paul," Horace said, as I approached.

"Hi, I'm Jessica, and this is Lori," one of them said.

They were Americans. As we talked for a while, we discovered they were in a program in Rome and also had a week off. I could tell Jessica liked me, so I concentrated on her. The trick would be to separate them. I asked her if she wanted to go to the bow of the ship to see the lights of the town ahead. She agreed. Horace winked at me as we left; I knew I had made the right move. It was going to be a short trip, so I had to work fast.

"You seem somewhat shy," I said.

"Just at first," she said.

"Did you ever kiss someone you had just met?" I said.

"I don't think so," she smiled.

"Do you want to kiss me?" I said.

"Maybe. I'll think about it," she said.

"I don't usually approach women that way, but I'm really attracted to you, and our trip is so short. I figured I wouldn't waste any time," I said.

"I'm attracted to you too," she said.

I tried to kiss her, but she turned her face, so I licked her neck and worked my way back to her mouth. She opened her lips gently, and our tongues melted into a delicious, long kiss. I slipped my arms around her and grabbed her ass. She pushed my hand away, but when I tried again, she left it there.

"Pretty aggressive aren't you?" she said.

"We have so little time," I said.

"What! Do you think you're going to fuck me on the train?" she laughed.

"No, no, of course not," I said.

I tried to put my hand between her legs, but she pushed me away again. She kept kissing me though. I figured that was enough for a while. Again, I grabbed her ass.

"Stop, Paul. What do you think you're doing?"

"What do you think I'm doing?" I laughed.

"I'm not going to fuck you right here!" she said.

"I'm sorry; let's just kiss," I said.

"Stop now. Let's just talk," she said.

"All right, I'm sorry," I said.

"You men only want one thing. What's wrong with you guys?" she asked.

"We're made that way," I said.

The ferry was slowly making its way to the other side. Jessica wanted to join the others, who were kissing as we approached. Horace was disgruntled when we suddenly appeared.

"Don't you two have something to do?" he said.

"We already did it," I said.

The four of us got talking again and everybody felt more comfortable. They had a different destination than we did, so I abandoned any fantasy of getting laid. We sat with them on the train and said goodbye a few hours later when they got off. Horace and I had decided to return to Catania where we had been before. We had three more hours of what was getting to be a painful train ride.

"Let's look for a hotel near the water. It'll be more beautiful," Horace said.

"It'll also be more expensive," I said.

"We'll find a cheap one," he said.

We walked along the waterfront for what seemed like hours until, finally, two blocks from the beach, we found a small pensione that was reasonable. We slept a long time, and then went out for dinner at a little pizza place nearby. We searched for a bar to get a cocktail, but there weren't any. Disappointed, and still tired, we walked back to the hotel and went to sleep. In the morning, we woke up refreshed and ready to go. The sun was up, so we decided to hang out at the beach. Even though it was relatively warm, nobody was there.

"What's wrong with this town?" Horace said.

"We should go back to Taormina. There's more going on there," I said.

"Good idea," he said.

Without hesitating, we returned to the pensione, packed our bags, and got on the train for Taormina.

Two hours later, we were in paradise. We walked around again looking for a hotel and found a cheap one way up the hill. We took a bus way down the mountain and hung out on the beach even though, again, there was hardly anyone there.

"We'll find some action tonight in this town," Horace said.

"I'm sure there are some women around," I said.

We ate near the beach, outdoors, and spotted a couple of

women eating nearby.

"They're Italian," I said.

"I wonder if they're on vacation from up North," Horace said. "It's your turn, Paulie. They probably don't speak any English."

I approached them and discovered that, sure enough, they were Italian. Knowing immediately that it would be more difficult to pick them up, I just introduced myself and pointed over to Horace, explaining we were on vacation. They were about nineteen or twenty. There was going to be no way we were getting those girls into bed. After a little more conversation, I told them we hoped to run into them again and left it at that.

Following lunch, we got some sun and went back to the hotel to sleep. The nightlife, unfortunately, was pretty dismal, but we did find one bar that had some women in it. We sat at a table, ordered some beer, and got into a conversation about our futures.

"How are you going to support yourself with this writing gig?" Horace said.

"I don't know yet. After I graduate this year, I think I'm just going to wait on tables and knock out the first one in a few months," I said. "After that, I'm either going to law school or into teaching."

"You should come down to North Carolina, stay with me and write. I can get you a job in a restaurant immediately," he said.

Just then, I noticed three women sitting together in the back of the bar who were laughing and having a great time.

"Check out those girls," I said.

Horace turned around casually, and got a good look at them.

"Not bad, but they don't look like Americans," he said.

"There are lots of Germans in this town," I said.

"You go up to them," he said.

I got up my courage and walked up to them. At first they looked oddly at me, but when I introduced myself, they seemed to relax and smile. Sure enough, they were German, but they all spoke English. I asked them if we could join them, but they declined politely. When I got back to our table, Horace said:

"You fucked it up, didn't you?"

"What do you want from me? I asked them if we could sit with them, and they said no; it's not my fault."

"Are they German?"

"Yeah, but they speak English."

"They do? We'll wait a while. Then I'll go up to them. I can't expect you to do a man's job." He laughed.

We had a few more beers to loosen up; then Horace walked up to them. He stood there looking confident, chatting them up, making them laugh every once in a while. Next, he motioned for me to come over and winked at me as I pulled up a chair. I sat next to a gorgeous blonde named Hanna, and I felt intimidated by her. She smiled and laughed so easily, I felt I would die if I didn't have her. I knew my chances were very slight, but Horace gave me courage.

"Where are you from?" she asked me.

"New York," I said, without explaining that I was from Upstate.

"What about you?" I said.

"A small town not far from Berlin," she said. "I'm at University."

After half an hour of chitchat, I asked her if she wanted to go for a walk in the moonlight. She agreed, which made my heartbeat increase. We excused ourselves and went out into the fresh air. It was a beautiful night, and the air coming off the sea smelled wonderful. I held her hand as we walked along the street, and I told her about my town and my friends. She had written some poetry; she was glad to recite it to me, what she could remember, and I thought it was pretty good. She was a sweetheart; I was definitely infatuated with her and had an irresistible urge to give her a kiss.

The two of us stood at a spot looking out over the sea, the moon reflecting on the water, and I kissed her.

"I really like you," I said.

"I like you too," she said.

I was afraid to kiss her again right away, but I did anyway, holding her close to me and pressing my tongue deep inside her mouth. Of course, I wanted to sleep with her, but I liked her so much, I was afraid to ask her to go back to my room with me.

"Want to walk some more?" I said.

We walked slowly, talking and laughing, her eyes sparkling under the streetlamps.

"Let's go this way," I said, guiding her toward my hotel.

Then I thought maybe it would be better to leave well enough alone, and set things up for the following night. As we approached the hotel, I asked her if she wanted to come in, and she agreed. I thought maybe I would get lucky, or at least have a good time trying. We sat on the bed and talked, holding hands and looking lovingly into each other's eyes. I kissed her and leaned back on the bed, my arms around her.

"Slow down," she said. "You're going too fast."

We talked some more; then I tried again. This time she was

more passionate, but she wouldn't let me put my hand up her skirt. She let me grab her ass though, so I kept fondling it until she got pretty hot. Then she pushed me away.

"That's enough," she said.

"Oh," I said, and moved away from her.

She wanted to go back to her friends, so we walked along the same street, looking out over the water, as if time didn't exist. I wanted that moment to last forever. Horace was pretty well lubricated when we arrived, and was entertaining the others. They wanted to go to bed, so we separated, and I went home. Horace didn't want to go to sleep right away, but I did. I went back to the hotel by myself and collapsed. In the morning, Horace was up before me; I couldn't figure out how he did it. He didn't have a hangover, was bright and cheery as usual, and wanted to go out and explore.

"This town has to be the most beautiful spot in the world," he said.

"A lot of interesting people have spent quite a bit of time here," I said, "D.H. Lawrence being my favorite."

We took the bus down to the waterfront and walked around for a long time. Horace and I were supposed to meet the women later, and I wanted to sleep more, so we went to the beach and just slept. That night the women were sitting in the same spot, and were glad to see us.

"I'm moving to Germany," Horace declared. "You have the loveliest women in the world."

"Italy's not bad either," Ingrid said.

"We have a greater variety in the States," I said.

"We might be going to the States next year," Horace said.

After an hour of drinking and talking, I asked Hanna if she wanted to go for a walk again, and she agreed. It was cloudy that night. The moon and stars were not out, but the lights from the town danced on the water. We sat on a park bench, drinking from a bottle of wine, holding each other closely.

"I think I'm in love with you," I said.

"You liar," she laughed. "You'll say anything to get into my pants."

"No, I wouldn't. You're beautiful, intelligent, funny, and very sweet," I said.

"I'm sure you have a girlfriend in Florence, and I bet you have one in the States too," she said.

"No, I don't," I said.

"You liar!" she said.

We held each other for a while, drinking our wine, kissing a little.

"Let's go to my hotel," I said.

"No, I don't think so," she said.

"Come on. I won't attack you," I said.

"Just for a little while," she said.

We walked arm in arm through the narrow streets, which were dimly lit by old streetlamps. I was glad I hadn't had too much to drink. I wanted to concentrate on getting her into bed, and she seemed pretty drunk. She even stumbled once, but I held on to her so she wouldn't fall. We were laughing at everything. The night seemed magical, and I was having a ball. I could tell she was horny too; she kept grabbing my ass.

"You have the nicest ass," she said.

"Yours isn't bad either," I said.

When we got to the hotel, we jumped on the bed and began kissing passionately. She was slobbering all over me, and I immediately put my hand between her legs, which she let me keep there. She started groaning, and I put her hand on my cock; she began massaging me. I tried to unzip her pants, but she pushed my hand away. I tried again several minutes later, and this time she let me. Her pants were so tight, I had trouble reaching down all the way to her pussy. Her cunt was so wet, my three fingers slid right inside. She arched her back and bit my tongue.

"Ow, that hurt," I said.

"Shut up and fuck me," she said, pulling her pants off.

She had the most beautiful legs and pussy I had ever seen. I dove in, head first, and licked her until she came.

"I want you inside me," she said, pulling me toward her. She was dripping wet, and my cock felt bigger than usual. I moved slowly at first; then increased my speed, until finally I was pounding her. She started to scream as I came inside her, and we started laughing when we heard somebody knocking on the wall. I collapsed next to her, and we kissed for a while, whispering intimate feelings to each other.

"You took advantage of me," I teased.

"You helpless child," she said.

We took a short nap, and then went back to the bar, but nobody was there. She decided to return to her hotel, and I went back to mine. I didn't wait for Horace to return. Instead, I went to sleep.

The next morning, Horace woke me up and gave me a cup of coffee. He had already been up for an hour and was anxious to find out what had happened the night before. I gave him most of the details, and he enjoyed every bit of it. We were supposed to meet the girls on the beach, but that would be later. I wanted to get something to eat. It felt great to have been fucked the night before. I had a big smile on my face.

We went to a café next door and ate some pastries. The day was warm, and the sun was out. I was looking forward to fucking Hanna again.

"Does Ingrid want to fuck you?" I asked Horace.

"I think so, but I couldn't separate her from Maria. They cling to each other like glue," he said.

"I'll take Maria with us. Then we'll drop her off at their hotel," I said.

"If you could do that, it would be great," he said.

We took the bus down to the beach, an hour or so before the girls were supposed to be there. We put our towels down and stripped down to our boxers, not having bathing suits. Again, there was no one on the beach, and we slept until the girls arrived.

"Wake up," Hanna said, shaking me.

"What are you girls up to?" Horace said.

"We want to go swimming," Ingrid said.

"Swimming? It's too cold," I said.

"No it's not. Come on. It'll be refreshing," she said.

Horace and I were not going to be dragged into the water, and just watched them swim. They were gorgeous in their suits, and I couldn't take my eyes off Hanna's body. Ingrid had a nice body too; when they sat down again next to us, we kept looking at their legs. We laughed the rest of the afternoon. The girls were really enjoying our company, and Horace was talking of nothing but sex. We left them around dinnertime, making our same appointment for the evening. Horace and I bought some food at a grocery store, trying to keep down our expenses. We went back to the hotel and stuffed our faces.

"I can't wait to fuck Hanna again tonight," I said.

"Don't count on it until it happens," he said.

"She fucked me last night. Why wouldn't she tonight?" I said.

"You can never tell about women. She might feel guilty, or that she made a mistake. You can never tell," he said. "If I were you, I would go easy on her," he added.

"We're only going to be here two more nights. Why wouldn't she just let herself go?" I said.

"She might," he said.

After eating, Horace and I went out to buy some beer. We wanted to get started early. We had a long, somewhat drunken, heartfelt talk about our pasts; one could not have put two more disparate stories together. I had had a great childhood, not a drink or a drug in high school, a member of many sports teams, and happy all the time. He had come from a dirt-poor family, with a crazy mother, and drank at an early age. I didn't know it at the time, but he was already a full-blown alcoholic.

"My father doesn't drink any more," he said, "but you can imagine raising seven children by yourself. He's a strong man in many ways, but not someone you can talk to. He expects things done a certain way, and that's it."

"I was raised by my mother after my eighth year, and she did a great job. There are three boys, and we were always involved in athletics. We hung out with good kids, and all went to college eventually, even though my older brother went into the navy first," I said.

After a while, we decided to go to a café to continue our talk and sit outside. The stars were out and just a sliver of moon. It was beautiful, and I gave a wistful sigh that our trip was almost over with. The yellowish lights along the streets reminded me of a painting by Van Gogh. There was romance in the air, and I was horny as hell. After a couple of hours of drinking coffee, we were sober and ready to meet the girls.

We got there before them, and Horace had placed enough doubt in my mind to wonder if they would show up at all.

"Try to get Maria away from Ingrid, would you?" Horace said. "I need to get laid."

"I'll try," I said.

Half an hour later, the girls showed up. Hanna was wearing a short red skirt with black stockings, looking incredibly sexy. The other two were wearing jeans, which showed off their tight bodies. I tried to get Maria to walk with Hanna and me, but it didn't work, and I knew Horace was upset. Hanna and I went to the same spot we had gone to the first night and sat overlooking the sea.

"This is when the moon is the most romantic," she said, pointing to the orange sliver in the sky.

I kissed her, moving my tongue ever so slowly over hers. She moaned gently and pulled me close to her. I already had a hard on.

"Will you write to me when you get back to Germany?" I said.

"Of course I will," she said.

"You can visit me in the States," I said, repeating things I had said to her before.

I wanted to go right to the hotel, but I remembered what Horace had said and sat kissing for a long time, whispering sweet nothings into her ear.

"I could really fall in love with you," I said.

"Don't start with me," she said.

"I know it's nearly impossible carrying on an overseas relationship, but it is possible," I said.

"You couldn't really fall in love with me. You just want to get into my pants again," she said.

"You can't blame me, can you?" I said.

"See what I mean?" she said.

"Let's go to the hotel anyway. We'll just talk. I promise," I said.

We walked slowly through the narrow streets, arm in arm, kissing every once in a while. There were only a few people walking around town, and I felt a million miles away from home. I really did like Hanna. She was everything a man could hope for, but she was convinced all I wanted was sex. The conquest is everything for the man, but I wanted to be intimate, to have her, own her, to have her think about me and love me. There was still some wine in our hotel room, so Hanna and I had a few drinks. We talked about Germany and Italy, and I told her about my life in the States.

Every once in a while I thought I really could fall in love with her, and I knew it would be painful to say goodbye. We kissed passionately, and my erection grew again. I wanted to fuck her in the worst way. I hoped that the wine would loosen her up a little, but I got some resistance. She let me rub her breasts over her shirt, but she wouldn't let me put my hand under it. I tried to rub her between her thighs, but she wouldn't let me do that either. After a while, I gave up.

"What's wrong, Hanna?" I said.

"I just don't want to do anything," she said.

"Why not?"

"I don't know; I just don't."

I was so frustrated; I started to feel angry, but knew, of course, it was just too bad for me. We left a few minutes later, and hardly talked all the way to her hotel. I kissed her goodnight and said goodbye, knowing I would never see her again.

Chapter Thirty-Three

Two days later, Horace and I boarded the train for Florence. I looked out the window wistfully at the orange groves and beautiful farmhouses. There weren't too many people traveling, so we could stretch out in our cabin and sleep most of the way there. Fourteen hours later, we arrived in Florence and took a taxi to my apartment. John was there and greeted us warmly.

"Hey guys, how was your trip? Are you hungry or tired?" he said.

"Neither. We slept most of the way and ate on the train," Horace said.

John wanted to hear all about our trip, so we gave him some of the highlights and left the rest to his imagination. He had had a great trip himself, but there wasn't any interesting sex to hear about.

"When is Jesse getting back?" I asked him.

"He's back already," he said.

"What about the women?" Horace said.

"They're all back too," John said.

"Are they coming over tonight?" I asked.

"Not tonight, but we can call them if you want to," John said.

"I'm sure your wife wants you home," he said to Horace.

"Let's have a reunion here," I said.

"Good idea," Horace said.

John called the girls, while Horace and I went out to buy

food. It felt great to be back in Florence, walking along the familiar streets and going to the market. It was warm that afternoon, and a lot of people were walking through the streets. We passed the statue of the David, and when I looked at him that time, he seemed to be pleased with himself for conquering another woman. He is sexy. There's no doubt about that. No woman would turn him down, or man for that matter, remembering Michelangelo's preference.

We bought all kinds of food. It was exciting to see the same vendors at the market. They asked us where we had been, and said they thought we had returned to the States.

"I'm going to hate leaving Italy," Horace said.

"I know what you mean," I said.

When we returned, Jesse and John were playing cards, and we were informed that the women would be over in a couple of hours.

"Who's coming?" were the first words out of my mouth.

"Melanie, Monica, and Jennifer," John said.

"Great," I said.

"You're going to get into trouble tonight," Horace said.

"Why do you say that?" I said.

"Because you were talking about Monica all the time on the trip, and Jennifer is going to get jealous," he said.

"Just don't say anything about me screwing Hanna. Okay?" I said.

"I'm not going to say anything!" he grinned.

We played cards for a couple of hours, waiting for the women to arrive, and we broke out the wine. Horace told some precious stories about the deep South that had us almost in tears. He seemed a different person in Italy. He was not nearly as wild as he portrayed himself, which made me suspicious about his stories. Finally, the girls showed up. Melanie and Monica insisted on cooking, giving Horace a break. Jennifer sat with the boys in the dining room and joined the card game.

"Tell me all about your trip, Paul," she said.

I told her how we changed our plans and stayed in Taormina the whole time. At one point, as I was telling her about the nightlife there, she shocked me.

"Did you get laid?" she asked.

"No, of course not," was my immediate response.

"I don't believe you," she said, "but I don't care either."

I think she could tell by my face that I was lying, but I really didn't care. We weren't getting off to a good start; I could feel a fight brewing for later, and I wasn't looking forward to it. Dinner was ready half an hour later; I was hungry as hell. I sat between Monica and Jennifer, and all I wanted to do was talk to Monica.

"How was France?" I asked her.

"Great. You know I didn't realize that Monet's water lilies were so big. They're incredible!" she said.

"What I find amazing is the variation on one theme; he painted so many colors from those waters," I said.

Jennifer wanted to say something, but Monica cut her off.

"Colors are subtle during the Renaissance, but not like the Impressionists," she said.

"I think it's also a movement from the portrayal of reality to the perception of reality, truly a modern movement," Jennifer said.

"That's true," I said.

"What would be the postmodern move then?" Horace said.

Everybody wanted to answer that question.

"Doubting one's own perception," Jennifer said.

"A total skepticism," Melanie said.

"Multiple contradictory perceptions," John said.

"The struggle between subjectivity and objectivity," I said.

"The decomposition of story and character," Jesse said.

"What's left?" Horace laughed.

"There will always be color and movement in painting," Monica said.

The conversation continued, and I could sense that Jennifer was getting irritated by all the attention I was giving Monica. After a while I decided to cool it with Monica and talk to Jennifer a bit more. She wasn't very receptive.

"Tell me about your trip," I said to her.

"There's really nothing to tell," she said.

I gave up after that and joined the mainstream of conversation. After dinner, Jennifer and I went into my room; I wasn't feeling too comfortable.

"You fucked somebody on your trip, didn't you?" she started right away.

"No, I swear I didn't," I said.

"I can tell by the look on your face; you look guilty as hell," she said.

"We're not married, Jennifer," I said.

That was absolutely the wrong thing to say.

"So you did fuck somebody! And we don't have to be married to be faithful to one another!"

"I fooled around with somebody; I didn't fuck her," I said.

"Same thing, you would have fucked her if she had let you!"

"Sex is meaningless to me; I don't have feelings for her, I have feelings for you," I said.

"You have more feelings for Monica," she said. "I think

we're through!"

"Come on, Jennifer. Every relationship goes through tough times. Don't give up on us," I said.

She wouldn't be consoled. She stormed out of the room and out of the apartment. I didn't even try to follow her. I decided to go to bed and not explain to the others what happened.

Several hours later, I heard everybody leave. I didn't sleep well. Jennifer's words echoed in my mind all night long. I only had two hours of sleep when I heard John or Jesse get into the shower. I felt like shit and wanted to sleep, but couldn't. So I dragged myself out of bed and made some coffee. John was in the kitchen.

"What did you say to Jen last night?" he said.

"She could tell I fucked a girl on vacation, but I really think she's jealous of Monica," I said. "She says we're through."

"What are you going to do?" he said.

"What can I do?"

"Tell her you're sorry and that you love her."

"I tried that," I said.

"She'll come around," he said.

"By then, I'll be back in the States," I said.

When I got to school, Horace was sitting in his seat with his usual grin on his face. I rolled my eyes, and he laughed. I ordered a double cappuccino. The smell and taste of the coffee made me feel better.

"What's up there, buddy?" he said.

"I think Jen and I are through," I said. "She's really pissed off this time. She's jealous of Monica."

"You can't blame her, can you?" he said.

"Whose side are you on?"

"I'm on my side," he said.

I drank my cappuccino quickly and tried to cheer up. I knew Horace would pull me out of my bad mood.

"You think I should try to get back together with her or let her go?" I said.

"Let her go. You're not in love, and there's only a few weeks left of school," he said.

"I guess you're right."

I skipped the first class and sat talking to Horace. It wasn't long before he had me laughing. A couple of coffees later, I started feeling better. After my second class, Horace and I took off for downtown to go to the market. The noise of the city was delicious. We bought quite a bit of food and headed back to my apartment. Nobody was home when we got there and Horace whipped up two plates of pasta.

"I want to get Monica into bed before the end of the semester, but I don't think she'll go for it," I said.

"Is she sleeping with anyone right now?" he asked.

"I don't think so," I said.

"You might have a chance, a slim one," he said.

"What should I say to her?" I said.

"There's not much you haven't already said to her," he said.

We got the cards out and played some rummy, waiting for John and Jesse to show up. It was starting to rain, and I was feeling pretty tired. After a few hands of cards, I told Horace that I had to take a nap. I slept for two hours. When I woke up, I found John, Jesse, George, and Horace playing pitch.

"There he is," George said.

"I feel better now," I said.

Several hours later, Horace cooked some chicken and pasta, but the women didn't come over. It was a bachelor's evening, and the talk got pretty raunchy. The wine flowed, and the laughter flowed just as quickly. I got pretty drunk and had it in my mind that I had to talk to Monica. Horace tried to dissuade me, but I was insistent. The first words out of her mouth after answering the phone were:

"You're drunk."

"I know," I said. "We're having a party."

"I don't want to talk to you when you're drunk," she said.

"I'm not that drunk," I said.

I wanted to tell her that I loved her and wanted to marry her, but I was chicken. Even being sauced didn't give me that kind of courage. I looked over and Horace had his hand on his face, expecting disaster.

"I want to be your boyfriend," I said.

"We've been through this," she said. "I'm going to hang up now. I'll talk to you tomorrow."

"No, don't hang up; I'll behave. How was your day. Tell me everything you did today," I said.

"I worked on a painting all day and went to the market," she said.

"How did the painting turn out?" I said.

"Fine. Listen, Paul, I've got to go," she said tensely.

"All right," I said and hung up.

"Good job," Horace said.

"What an idiot I am," I said.

"She doesn't care. Don't worry about it," John said.

We went back to drinking and playing cards. I soon forgot about the phone call.

In the morning though, when I woke up, I immediately thought about Monica and the ass I made out of myself. I was hung over and in a foul mood. Horace was sleeping on the couch. I listened to him snore as I made some espresso. It was a bright day. I wished I had felt better, so I could enjoy the sunshine. The coffee tasted good. It woke me up, and after a while, I started feeling a little better. I had three shots of espresso and was wide-awake when Horace began to stir.

"Get your ass out of bed," I said to him.

"Leave me alone," he said. "I'm getting up."

I took a shower and waited for Horace to have his coffee and get dressed.

"Let's take the bus," I said.

"Oh, I don't feel much like walking either," he said.

When we got to school, Monica and Melanie were sitting in the café chatting. I could feel myself turning red as we sat down. Monica had a smug smile on her face when I looked at her.

"Hi, Paul." She giggled.

Melanie was smiling too. I didn't know what to say, so I didn't say anything for a minute. I was hoping Horace would say something helpful.

"I heard you guys had a great time last night?" Melanie said.

"It was all right," Horace said.

"You didn't get enough sleep," Melanie said to her husband.

"I'll take a nap later," he said.

"I feel great," Monica said.

I tried not to frown but did anyway. I went up to the bar and ordered two cappuccinos. I was getting into a worse mood.

When I sat down again, Monica had a more empathetic look on her face.

"I feel like shit," I said.

"We can tell," Monica said. "I won't hold that phone call against you."

"Thanks."

"Actually, I thought it was pretty funny," she said.

"Strange sense of humor," I said.

"Forget about it," Horace said.

"I didn't mean it quite that way, Paul," Monica said.

"I knew what you meant; I'm just not in a good mood," I said.

"It's already forgotten," she said.

A few minutes later, I dragged my ass to class and fell asleep at my desk. I woke up at the end of the period, but I felt better. I decided not to stay for my other classes and talked Horace into leaving with me. We went to the market as usual and bought some food, but I was anxious to return to the apartment and take a long nap.

"I think I really fucked it up with Monica this time," I said.

"Maybe, but she really likes you; why, I don't know, but she was looking at you very lovingly this morning," he said.

We were walking along the river, and I noticed more and more fishermen were frequenting the downtown area. I was thinking how much I would miss Florence, and I wondered how long it would be before I could return.

"I'm only going to be here two more weeks; I've got to take another shot at her," I said. "I might even look her up when I get back to the States."

"You say that about all the women," he said.

When we got to the apartment, I went right to bed. I slept

for two to three hours and felt great when I woke up. Horace and John were playing cards and drinking wine, but I decided to stay away from the wine for a change. A few minutes later, George showed up with Jesse. We all played cards for a while, until Horace decided he wanted to start cooking.

"Are any women coming over tonight?" George asked.

"I don't think so," John said. "By the way, Horace, Melanie wants you home tonight."

"Okay," Horace said.

Horace made a pasta sauce with everything in it: vegetables, meat, spices. It tasted like an American sauce because he put sugar and vinegar in it. He made enough for an army, and it was delicious. After dinner, the boys played cards, while I slipped into the bedroom to call Monica. Horace yelled:

"Don't make a jackass out of yourself!"

I was nervous and hadn't a clue as to what I would say.

"Hello?" she said.

"Hi, Monica; it's Paul."

"Hi, baby. What's up?"

"I thought I'd call you sober to make up for last night," I said.

"I told you it's forgotten," she said.

"Listen, why don't we go out for dinner this weekend, just the two of us," I said.

"That would be great," she said.

"Okay. I'll talk to you later."

"Bye," she said.

I had wanted to tell her that I really cared for her, but hadn't had the balls to do it. I figured I would do it that weekend. The guys razzed the hell out of me when I went back to the dining room, but I felt great. Then I had a glass of wine. It seemed forever until Saturday arrived, and I was pretty nervous, even though Monica and I had been out alone several times.

When I got to her apartment, she was still getting ready, so she served me a glass of wine, and had me sit at the kitchen table. I drank the wine too fast and filled the glass again.
 "Where are we going?" she said from her bedroom.
 "I thought we'd go to that trattoria by the river. Remember the one we went to a few months ago?" I said.
 "Great idea," she said.
 I thought about walking into her bedroom and catching her naked, but, of course, I didn't. When she came out, she looked fabulous. She had tight jeans on with a simple white blouse and pearls.
 "You look great!" I said.
 "Thanks."
 We walked along the river, talking, and I felt in love. We held hands for a while and laughed easily. It was busy when we got to the restaurant, but we didn't have to wait long. We ordered a full carafe of wine and just pasta because we didn't have much money.
 "I'm leaving right after school ends," I said.
 "I heard that. I'm staying through the summer; I'm going to miss you," she said.
 "I'm going to miss you too."
 After a few glasses of wine, we ordered another carafe. I was starting to get drunk, and so was she. The pasta kept us sober for a while, but we kept on drinking after the meal. This was our goodbye. When we left the restaurant, we were laughing so hard we could hardly walk. She lived alone, so we decided to go back to her apartment. I put my arm around her as

238

we walked and told her at one point that I loved her.

"I love you too," she said.

I was sure she would make love to me that night. She seemed in the perfect mood. I kissed her on the cheek as we stood by the river and admired the lights dancing on the water. Then I kissed her on the lips and slipped my tongue gently inside her mouth. She opened her mouth and pushed her tongue against mine. When we pulled away, we both giggled.

"Why couldn't we have started this way months ago?" I said.

"Because," she said.

"Good reason," I said.

We walked very slowly back to her apartment and kissed every so often along the way. Her kisses were making me hard. There wasn't much furniture in the apartment, which consisted of two rooms and a balcony. I sat on the bed, pulling her down with me. We stretched out and began kissing with intense passion. I grabbed her ass, which I had been wanting to do since the day I had met her. I was hard as a rock. I began massaging her breasts outside her shirt and could feel her nipples getting erect. When I put her hand between my legs, she pulled it away.

"Come on, honey," I said.

She didn't say anything, but I knew if I got her hot enough, she would come through. I put my hand under her shirt, which she let me do, and rubbed her small breasts.

"I love you," I said.

"I love you too," she said.

I tried putting my hand down her pants, but she wouldn't let me do that either. I was getting frustrated.

"Come on, baby," I said.

"This is as far as we're going," she said.

I attempted to go further, but got nowhere. Instead, I settled for kissing her and rubbing her; but without knowing it, I was angry.

"This is our last time together. Don't you want something to remember me by?" I said.

"I will always remember you," she said.

A few minutes later, I left in a huff. I was perfectly sober by the time I got home and went straight to bed.

Chapter Thirty-Four

I woke up still feeling angry and frustrated, but I let it all go as I took a long, hot shower. I made a double espresso after I got dressed, and sat down with John for a while.

"She didn't go for it," I said.

"What did you expect?"

"She told me she loved me."

"That doesn't mean she's going to fuck you," he said.

"I was so close."

"Yet so far." He laughed

We talked for a few minutes then decided to go for a run. We jogged toward the outskirts of the city, which was very quiet that Sunday morning. After our run, I felt a lot better. The next day we began the last week of school.

Horace was sitting in the café talking to Monica when I arrived. I felt a little uncomfortable, but I sat down with them anyway.

"What's up, guys?" I said.

"You, Paulie," Horace said.

"Are you still mad at me?" Monica said.

"No, of course not."

"I'm glad," she said.

I ordered a double cappuccino and felt more at ease because of Monica's comments.

"I caught up on my sleep yesterday," I said.

"So did I," Monica said. "Well, I have to go to my studio.

I've got to finish my last project by the end of the week."

"Bye," I said, feeling slightly relieved that she was leaving.

"She told me about Saturday night," Horace said.

"No big deal," I said.

"You'll have to pursue her in the States, that's all," he said.

"That seems pretty far-fetched right now," I said.

"You never know," he said.

We chatted for a while longer. Then I went to class. I had to study hard that week to catch up on my work, so we all laid low until the night before I flew back home. It was a Friday night, and we had planned a large dinner party.

All our friends were at the party, and we broke out the wine early. Horace kept refilling everyone's glass, and it wasn't long before we were pretty tipsy.

"Here's a toast to Paul, who is leaving tomorrow; Italy will never be the same," Horace said.

"I'm surprised they're going to let him back into the States," John said.

Horace began cooking. He made two whole baked chickens and tons of pasta. He put some wine in with the chickens and some in the pasta sauce. I waited until Monica sat down, and then sat next to her. On my other side was John. George was there, Ellen, Melanie, Jesse, Patricia, and, of course, Horace. The conversation got loud after a while, and Horace made it worse.

When the food was ready, we all began to eat, and the conversation died down to a dull roar.

"What are you going to do when you get back, Paul?" Melanie said.

"I'm going to law school, I think," I said.

"You should come down south to see us," she said.

"Maybe I will," I said.

Little did I know that the following year I would decide not to go to law school and would go south instead to stay with Horace and Melanie. When I stayed with them in North Carolina, I wrote my first novel.

"What are you going to do, John, when you go back?" Horace said.

"I may stay here a while; I've got a job at a restaurant for the summer, and who knows what will happen by fall?" he said.

"Patricia, what about you?" Melanie said.

"I'm going back to school too," she said.

"I'm starting a breakfast restaurant," Horace said, "twenty-four hours, three shifts; I'll make a ton of money."

I had nostalgic feelings for the States, and I was anxious to return. I wished we could all move back together and continue our parties. Having been in Italy for the year had changed my perspective radically. I had a feeling I wouldn't go to law school. All I wanted to do was write my first novel, even though I had no idea what I would write about. I didn't know Monica would end up in Syracuse a year later. It was a very pleasant surprise.

We partied late into the night, and all of us had too much to drink. I wanted to talk to Monica privately, but I didn't get the opportunity. I flirted with all of the girls, thinking that I would never see any of them again. I went to bed very late, but went right to sleep. I dreamt of Monica, but it ended badly. She even rejected me in my dreams.

The next morning, I woke up early with a hangover and took several aspirins. I had packed the day before. It was a couple of hours before my train was leaving. I knew John and

Jesse weren't going to see me off. We had already said our goodbyes. I made some coffee and took a shower. As I was drinking my coffee, I looked out the window and pondered some of my fond memories of Italy. I thought mostly about the times Horace and I had together. It was a special friendship. He was and still is one of the most interesting people I have ever met. I remember distinctly the light that morning. It was soft and orange, a sweet light, and I felt nostalgic for the beautiful city.

    I called for a taxi, and made myself another espresso. The birds seemed to be saying goodbye, but even stronger than my nostalgia for Italy was my excitement for returning to the States. I was anxious to see my family and figured that I would work at summer camp again near Lake George, one of the most beautiful spots in the world. When I got into the taxi, I took one last look at our building and waved goodbye. The ride through the city was rapid. I hardly had a chance to see anything. Before I knew it, I was at the train station. As the train pulled out of the city, I looked with pleasure and pain at the lovely surrounding hills, knowing that it wouldn't be long before I returned.